W9-AXN-052

PRAISE FOR *GODZILLA RETURNS*

"A HIGH-SEA ADVENTURE WORTHY OF TOM CLANCY...THOROUGHLY CONSTRUCTED BATTLE SEQUENCES...WONDERFULLY CRAFTED PROSE...FAST-PACED, TIGHTLY WRITTEN, AND COMPELLING.... if readers are willing to look beneath the surface, they'll find an homage to Herman Melville's *Moby-Dick*. Cerasini's narrator, Brian Shimura, is a stand-in for Ishmael, Captain Ahab is split between monster experts Admiral Willis and Dr. Nobeyama, the harpooner Buntaro is Queequeg—and that makes the 'King of the Monsters' a new Moby-Dick....*Godzilla Returns* is an astounding debut of a new series."

—Joe Mauceri, *World of Fandom*

"THE ACTION SEQUENCES ARE FAST-PACED AND DEVASTATINGLY POWERFUL. For the first time, G-fans are faced with what it would be like to be a tank commander or a jet fighter pilot in combat with Godzilla....*Godzilla Returns* is a welcome addition to every Godzilla enthusiast's collection. Hopefully, it will become number one of an entire series of similar novels."

—J. D. Leeds, *G-Fan*

PRAISE FOR GODZILLA!

GODZILLA™

RETURNS

by Marc Cerasini

Random House Sprinters™

Random House 🏠 New York

Special acknowledgment: "Go, go, Godzilla," from the song "Godzilla" by Donald Roeser. Copyright © 1977 Sony/ATV Tunes LLC: All rights administered by Sony/ATV Music Publishing, 8 Music Square West, Nashville, TN 37203. All Rights Reserved. Used by Permission.

A RANDOM HOUSE SPRINTER PUBLISHED BY RANDOM HOUSE, INC.

Library of Congress Catalog Card Number: 96-67480

ISBN: 0-679-88221-9
IL: 14 and up
First Sprinter Edition: November 1996

Printed in the United States of America
10 9 8 7 6 5 4 3 2

To my father, who called me away from my toys to watch my first Godzilla movie on television—way back in 1960.

Thanks, Dad

GODZILLA™

RETURNS

> *"If I'd known where this would all lead,*
> *I would have become a watchmaker."*
>
> —Albert Einstein, shortly after the
> detonation of the first hydrogen bomb

CHAPTER 1

DEATH ON THE HIGH SEAS

May 3, 1996, 4:53 P.M.
The Pacific Ocean

The sky was slate gray and overcast. It was late afternoon, and the sun struggled to break through the thick cloud cover. The wan light tinted the ocean a dark green. Dirty white foam capped the rolling waves.

Because this barren patch of water was so far from land, no bird flew in the sky. No fish or whale broke the surface. No living thing was visible.

But suddenly the silhouette of an immense creature appeared just beneath the surface. Eerie blue flashes of ghostly radiance danced along the shadowy figure under the water—water that began to churn and bubble with tremendous heat.

Then the ocean itself began to ripple. Three parallel rows of huge, irregular bone spikes cut through the waves. They were massive, serrated, and definitely reptilian. Charcoal gray in the center, they faded to a bony white color at the edges. The spikes clacked and clattered together like monstrous steel plates.

A muffled roar bellowed from beneath the ocean's surface, and neon blue lights rippled across the three rows of spikes. The intense heat they gave off turned the ocean around them to steam in an instant.

Then they slowly sank beneath the surface. Blue incandescence shimmered deep under the water until the silhouette finally vanished.

In the ageless Pacific, under a sun that is more than a billion years old, similiar reptiles were once a common sight—four hundred million years ago.

Today, only one remains.

Captain First Rank Alexei Sterenko dropped the pen onto the map table and clicked off the overhead light. He rubbed his tired eyes and yawned.

Done, he thought.

Sterenko reached for his cup of tea, but found that it had gone cold. In the darkness of his cabin, he listened to the throb of the pumps, the hum of the reactor, the muffled voices of men. These were sounds he was accustomed to, sounds he had learned to love—the quiet sounds of a Russian *Akula*-class nuclear submarine on patrol in hostile waters.

And now we are going home.

It had been a long tour of duty. A few weeks ago, Captain Sterenko and his hundred-man crew had been watching and recording China's annual military exercises off the coast of Taiwan.

The Chinese test-fired missiles and cannons and sent aircraft on mock attacks against the island of

Taiwan. This made the government of Taiwan angry, and tensions were high between the two countries.

For the Russians, it was a chance to watch the Chinese Navy in action and gather valuable intelligence.

After observing the exercises, Captain Sterenko and his crew headed for nearby Okinawa. They spent another few days listening to the radio transmissions from the American base located there. The Cold War was over, and the United States was no longer the enemy—technically. Yet the Russians still watched the Americans, and the American Navy still followed the Russians.

In truth, not much had changed, Sterenko thought. But the urgency was gone now that Russia and the United States didn't have nuclear arsenals pointing at each other.

Sure, we're one big happy world now, Sterenko mused.

At last the mission was over, and Captain Sterenko felt a wave of sadness. The truth of it was that part of him did not want to return home to Russia. His wife was five years dead, his children grown and on their own. He had nothing back home—nothing but confusion and economic chaos. Since the Communists had fallen from power, uncertainty was all the Russians had.

Uncertainty and fear.

Not like out here, on duty, Sterenko thought. *Here there is order. Each man knows his duty and does it.*

There are no surprises at sea.

"Captain Sterenko." A voice crackled over the sub's intercom.

Sterenko reached out and flipped the switch. "Yes?"

"First Mate Vossolov asks that you report to the bridge immediately. We have spotted an unidentified object on our instruments."

Sterenko recognized the urgent voice. It was Mikail Ivanovich, the young man who was manning the sonar.

A good seaman, but excitable, Sterenko thought. *He probably spotted a pod of whales.*

Captain Sterenko rose and made his way down the narrow corridors to the command deck.

When Sterenko stepped onto the bridge, First Mate Marko Vossolov saluted and relinquished the command chair.

"What's going on?" Sterenko asked, returning the salute.

"Sir," said Ivanovich, the sonar man, "we have a strange object on our scopes. It's moving parallel with us and matching our speed."

"Is it an American submarine?" Captain Sterenko asked the young man. "Or one of the new *Yuushio-*class submarines the Japanese Self-Defense Force is deploying?"

Ivanovich shook his head. "No, sir," he replied. "I've never seen anything like this before. This object's sound signature is unique—it is not on our tapes."

"*Everything* is on our tapes,"Vossolov said confidently. The Russian Navy had a recording of every type of underwater sound, from American subs to natural underwater phenomena.

Sterenko looked at his first mate. Vossolov shrugged his shoulders and smiled at the young sonar man's zeal. Captain Sterenko walked over to the sonar screen and peered at it over Ivanovich's shoulder. His eyes widened when he saw the blip on the screen.

"It has not reacted to our sonar probe?" Sterenko asked. Ivanovich shook his head. *That's odd*, Sterenko thought. *If it's another ship, it should have reacted to our sonar sweep....It must be fish, or perhaps whales.*

"Are you sure there are no whale sounds?" Sterenko demanded. "That's much too big to be a single object. It has to be a pod of whales...or a huge school of tuna, perhaps?"

"No, sir," Ivanovich stated flatly. "That's a single, solid object. And look at the radiation sensors."

The captain peered over the sonar man's shoulders again. There was some residual radiation coming from the object.

Captain Sterenko picked up a spare set of headphones and put them on. He listened to the sounds of the ocean outside the *Akula*'s hull. His face grew more puzzled.

"There's no sound of metallic pumps or engines...just a steady thumping that sounds like... like a giant's heartbeat."

Sterenko looked down at Ivanovich. "Is it still following us?" he asked.

"Yes, sir," the young man replied, wiping sweat from his forehead. "It's behind us and portside. The object is still matching our course and speed."

Captain Sterenko pulled the headphones from his head. "Then let's *change* our course and speed," he said with a confidence he did not feel. Sterenko turned back to his first mate.

"Sound red alert."

"Sound red alert!" Vossolov repeated, hitting the alarm button.

Klaxons began to blare throughout the ship. The fluorescent lights dimmed and the red crash lights came on. They illuminated the submarine's bridge with an eerie scarlet glow.

Sterenko turned to another man on the bridge.

"Helmsman," he barked. "Take us down to five hundred feet. Increase speed to forty knots."

"Aye, Captain," the helmsman answered.

The *Akula* shot forward in the water. The nose of the bullet-shaped ship tilted and the submarine slipped deeper into the Pacific Ocean.

Sterenko watched Ivanovich at the sonar screen.

"Sir," the young man spoke after a moment, "the object has changed course. It's matching our speed. No! It's going faster." Ivanovich was tense now, and his fear was contagious. Everyone on the *Akula*'s bridge was nervous as they listened to the sonar man.

"The object is passing us. It's moving ahead of us. I—I can't believe how fast it is going! Its speed is...impossible."

"Calm down, Ivanovich!" Sterenko barked. "I want information, not opinions!"

Ivanovich nodded. He began to sweat again as his eyes followed the blip on the screen.

"It's seventeen hundred meters in front of us now, Captain, and moving away," Ivanovich reported. Then his head jerked. "Wait!" he cried. "It's slowing down."

Ivanovich looked up from the sonar screen. His eyes were wide. "Captain, the object is directly in front of us. It's blocking our way!"

"All stop!" Sterenko cried. He turned to Vossolov. "Order the torpedo room to ready tubes one and two!"

As the first mate passed along the command to the weapons room, everyone on the bridge grew more tense. They'd gone from a peacetime intelligence mission to armed conflict in a few brief minutes.

But armed conflict with *what?*

The officers and men on the bridge exchanged nervous glances. They could feel the boat slowing. Seconds later, the *Akula* was at a dead stop. So was the unidentified object in front of them. The bridge was silent now, except for the hum of electronic instruments.

"Captain!" Ivanovich cried, his voice shattering the tense stillness. "The object is moving again. It's made a 180-degree turn and is heading for us on a collision course!"

Sterenko didn't hesitate. "Launch torpedoes one and two!"

"Torpedoes launched!" First Mate Vossolov answered. The *Akula* shuddered twice as the two anti-submarine torpedoes left their tubes and raced toward the target. Each torpedo had a computer guidance system and was packed with enough explosives to sink an American *Los Angeles*-class submarine.

Sterenko watched the sonar screen over Ivanovich's shoulder.

"The object is still moving closer," Ivanovich cried again. "Sixteen hundred meters…fifteen hundred meters…fourteen…"

"Five seconds to impact," the first mate interrupted.

Exactly five seconds later, the *Akula* was rocked as the two torpedoes detonated. The bridge was shaken as the force of the explosion slammed against the submarine's titanium hull.

"Direct hit! Both torpedoes!" Ivanovich announced before his sonar screen went white. During the four seconds that the submarine was buffeted by the explosions, the sonar was useless. Those seconds seemed like an eternity to Sterenko. Finally, the sonar screen cleared.

"Captain!" Sonarman Ivanovich shouted. "It's still out there! The object is still coming. Nine hundred meters…eight hundred…"

"Take evasive action!" Sterenko screamed. "Right full rudder!"

The helmsman jerked the sub's controls. The *Akula* turned to the starboard, but it wasn't fast enough.

"It's almost on us, sir!" Ivanovich cried.

Just then, the entire submarine shuddered as over six hundred tons of force struck it. The submarine spun like a balloon on a string. Men and machinery were tossed about. Systems shorted out in showers of sparks. Collision alarms went off all over the ship. The hull was ruptured in a dozen places. Even the bridge began to fill with water.

"Damage report!" Captain Sterenko cried.

"Captain!"Vossolov answered. "The nuclear reactor has been damaged. It is leaking radiation. We must surface immediately!"

"Blow the ballast tanks!" Sterenko commanded, though he knew it was probably too late. The submarine had already lost hull integrity. The *Akula* was taking on far too much water.

Sterenko had trained his crew well. The men did their best to save the ship. They sealed watertight hatches and cut off the reactor from the rest of the ship. As the power died, the emergency lights flickered and went out.

Far from the bridge, near the center of the hull, the submarine was rocked by a secondary explosion that blew a ten-foot hole in the hull. It was a mortal wound. The boat dipped nose-down, and Sterenko felt the dying shudders of the *Akula*.

He turned and stared into the eyes of First Mate Vossolov.

"Launch the distress beacon," Sterenko said calmly. Vossolov reached out and flipped a switch. Then the *Akula* shuddered for a third and final time as something huge grabbed hold of it and began to squeeze.

Sterenko was dashed against a console as sparks leaped from it. He tried to hold on, but the force of the impact was too much. Sterenko collapsed to the deck.

He lay still. There was nothing he could do. Something had reached out from the ocean and destroyed them. Not knowing what it was troubled Sterenko, but only vaguely. He listened helplessly to the death screams of a hundred men.

His men.

Then Captain Sterenko and the rest of the crew heard it—the terrible roar of an incredibly gigantic beast of prey.

Suddenly, the damaged hull of the *Akula* split in half. Millions of gallons of ocean water rushed into the superheated reactor core and instantly turned to steam.

The resulting explosion was horrible. The superheated steam ripped the submarine to pieces. Chunks of the vessel and its contents were scattered along the ocean floor for miles. A huge steam bubble erupted on the ocean's surface.

Even though the core of the submarine's reactor stayed intact through the explosion, radioactive material leaked from it and spilled into the water as it slowly sank.

Nearby, the mysterious creature that had destroyed the submarine fed on that radiation.

It fed and grew stronger.

May 3, 1996, 5:05 P.M.
The United States naval base
Naha Harbor, Okinawa

Around the American base at Okinawa, the sound of the dying Russian submarine was picked up by hundreds of sound-sensitive devices that lined the ocean floor. These instruments constantly monitored submarine activity in the waters around the military base. They were the first line of defense against secret attacks.

The Navy officers monitoring the area noticed an increase in radioactivity in the same area as the sound disturbance. Experts and intelligence officers later agreed that a nuclear submarine had died out there. Probably a Russian *Akula*-class vessel. Likely an accident—though one of the U.S. Navy sonar men who listened to the tape over and over again swore he could hear the sound of a collision.

Others weren't so sure.

But there was *another* sound that everyone who listened to the tape heard clearly. It was a strange sound, not so easily explained. It sounded like the roar of a huge beast.

But that was ridiculous, everyone decided.

Helicopters and U.S. Navy rescue ships were immediately dispatched to the area. They found some debris floating on the surface—clothing, bits of soggy paper, broken plastic and wood, a huge oil slick. They also found some evidence of residual radiation. Searchers even found a corpse or two that the sharks had not yet torn to pieces.

There were no survivors.

CHAPTER 2

OUR MAN IN TOKYO

May 12, 1998, 7:16 P.M.
New Tokyo International Airport
Narita, Japan

Brian Shimura warily scanned the crowded glass-and-steel terminal building. After a moment, he sighed with relief.

Well, at least it looks like an airport, he thought.

Arriving in Tokyo, Japan, for the first time, Brian wasn't sure just what to expect. He'd heard so much about the sprawling Japanese capital—the most modern city in the world—that a cityscape out of *The Jetsons* probably wouldn't have surprised him. So far, however, New Tokyo International Airport looked a lot like every other airport he'd ever been in.

And that's a relief, he mused.

Brian had already gone through customs. A polite man wearing a spotless blue uniform and white gloves stamped his passport and welcomed him to Japan with a bow. Brian bowed back, but later thought that he probably shouldn't have. In

Japan, bowing was a sign of respect to your social superior. Was the customs official his "superior"? Brian didn't know. The whole concept took some getting used to.

Slinging his carry-on bag over his shoulder, Brian set off in search of the baggage area. He spotted a sign with the international symbol—a picture of a suitcase—and an arrow pointing where to go. But as he stepped into the corridor, he smacked right into an old man heading rapidly in the opposite direction.

"I'm sorry," Brian quickly muttered in English. The old man smiled and bowed. Brian, remembering his orientation brochure, bowed too.

"Sumi-masen," he apologized again, this time in passable Japanese.

The old man smiled, bowed once more, and hurried off. Brian was about to step into the corridor again when he noticed that pedestrian traffic was moving in an orderly fashion—and he was walking the wrong way! Flustered, he halted, switched lanes, and headed in the opposite direction.

A group of Japanese girls in school uniforms watched him with amusement. When they realized he'd spotted them, they covered their mouths and giggled. Then they hurried away.

Brian was sure they were laughing at him.

He tried not to care. Instead, he forged ahead. Eventually he found the baggage claim area. The huge steel carousel was already moving, spilling out brown, black, green, and blue suitcases. As he searched for his belongings, another man in a trim uniform and spotless white gloves touched his shoulder. Brian smiled as the man checked his baggage claim ticket—then handed Brian his most precious possession.

Brian looked over his surfboard. No nicks or scratches. The wax was still shiny. He bowed to the airline official and thanked him. The man bowed back and hurried off.

In a few moments, Brian had gathered the rest of his luggage. It was too much to carry alone, but he saw no porters around. As he pondered his next move, he felt another tap on his shoulder.

He turned and faced a tall, skinny American teenager with wavy brown hair. The guy wore a sport jacket, tie, and blue jeans.

"You must be the Big Kahuna," the American said, smiling as he stuck out his hand. "I'm Nick Gordon, INN science correspondent in training."

"Hi," Brian said happily. "I'm—"

"Brian Shimura," Nick interrupted. "I know. I've been sent here by the boss man to pick you up."

"Oh," Brian said, shaking his hand. "I knew someone was meeting me, but I thought you would have gotten here sooner."

"I'm always late," Nick said, not offended. "As my roommate, you'll have to get used to that."

Roommate? Brian thought with surprise. It hadn't occurred to him that he would have one—but then why should interning at Independent News Network be any different than college?

"Surf's up, Shimura," Nick said, breaking into his thoughts. "Let's go."

After grabbing some of Brian's luggage, Nick led him to the escalators. As they headed down two levels, Nick gave Brian his own unique orientation lecture.

"Do you speak Japanese?" Nick asked.

"Not very well yet," Brian replied sheepishly.

"Doesn't really matter," Nick told him. "The language in the newsroom is English. And we interns don't get to do much field work. But it's a shame you don't know the lingo better—there are places *you* can go that *I* can't."

"What do you mean?"

"Simple," Nick stated. "You look Japanese. I'm just a *gaijin*—a foreigner. People here in Japan would be more likely to trust you."

"I see," Brian said.

"How much money do you have?" Nick asked.

Brian was taken aback. "Well…"

"You'll need lots of it," Nick continued. "Tokyo ain't cheap. But the network provides a suite and three squares a day—American food, mostly—in the corporate cafeteria. That saves us some money."

Nick glanced down at his wristwatch. "We'll get back to headquarters too late to get dinner tonight, though. Hope you're not hungry!"

Nick continued to rattle on until Brian finally interrupted him. "Where are we going?" he asked.

"We're taking the train to downtown Tokyo," Nick informed him. "An INN van will meet us at Tokyo Station."

"Can't we just get a taxi?" Brian asked.

"My, we *are* spoiled," Nick replied.

"It's not that," Brian shot back. "It's just that I have all this luggage…"

"Which won't fit in an airport cab," Nick interrupted again. "And they *surely* aren't going to have enough room for your surfboard. Anyway, the trip downtown in a cab'll cost about three hundred U.S. dollars."

Brian's eyes widened in shock. "Three hundred bucks!"

"Still want that taxi?" Nick deadpanned. "I didn't think so," he said when Brian did not reply.

"So, are we taking a bullet train, a monorail, or what?" Brian asked, surrendering to Nick's obvious experience.

"Nah," Nick said. "Just an ordinary train—the Narita Limited Express. Green Car!—that means first class. We'll be in the heart of Tokyo in under an hour."

By the time Brian reached Tokyo, his head was spinning. There was so much to learn, and his new roommate wasn't much help. Nick's rapid-fire delivery of detailed information only confused him. To slow down the pace of new data, Brian had tried to engage Nick in personal conversation.

"Time enough for that later, old chum," Nick had replied, before launching into another lecture about Tokyo architecture.

At Tokyo Station, a huge brick building with a giant, ultramodern department store at one end, Nick bundled Brian's suitcases onto a pushcart and led him to the exit. Outside, an INN van with a Japanese driver was waiting for them. In minutes, they had loaded the van and were negotiating Tokyo traffic.

"It's late, so rush hour is probably over. We'll

take Expressway Number One, then switch to Two," Nick informed Brian. "In a little while we'll be in the Roppongi district—your home away from home for the next three months."

"I thought we were staying in Tokyo itself," Brian asked, momentarily confused.

"Roppongi is *part* of Tokyo, sort of like a suburb," Nick replied. "The city is divided into prefectures—there's Minato-ku, Meguro-ku, Setagaya-ku…"

Brian zoned out again. As Nick talked on, Brian stared out of the window at the sprawling, bustling, brightly lit city. He liked what he saw. Here he was, thousands of miles from his California home, in the land of his ancestors…in the city where his father had been born. But Tokyo wasn't anything like the city his father described. It was so much…*more!*

Along the way, Nick showed him some places of interest. "There's the Imperial Palace Gardens," he said, pointing to a beautifully manicured area of parkland and stone walls. A little while later, Brian spotted a huge orange-red steel framework structure that looked like a knockoff of the Eiffel Tower in Paris.

"That's Tokyo Tower," Nick told him. "It's huge. You can see it from our balcony."

As they drove through increasingly thick traffic, Nick pointed out embassies, nightspots, and shrines. Brian was impressed by Tokyo's size, and by its busy sidewalks. Every street, every alley was jammed with people.

"Is Tokyo like this all the time?" Brian asked, gesturing to the crowds.

"We're lucky," Nick said. "Roppongi is an exclusive area—foreign dignitaries, corporate heads, fashionable entertainers, politicians, they all flock here. It's one of Tokyo's centers for nightlife…and we get to live there rent-free. After we get you home, we'll change clothes and go clubbing!"

The van turned the corner and Nick pointed to a huge communications facility topped by antennas, satellite dishes, and microwave towers.

"There's TV Asahi—sometimes we tape there. INN headquarters is right up the street," Nick said. A minute later, as the van pulled up to the curb, Nick pointed again. "Here we are!" he announced.

Brian climbed out of the van and looked up at his new home. The Independent News Network Building was a twenty-story ultramodern glass-and-steel office building. But Brian soon realized that Nick was pointing to the structure next to it—an older building that looked like a small apartment complex, complete with tiny balconies.

"Your new home," Nick said, beaming.

Brian stepped out of the van as the driver began to unload the luggage. Soon he was joined by another man in a security guard's uniform. Everyone grabbed a suitcase. Brian carried his surfboard under one arm.

"Come on," Nick said to Brian. "I'll carry you across the threshold."

Nick made Brian take his shoes off before he entered their rooms. "Japanese custom," he said. The suite consisted of two tiny bedrooms connected to an equally small living room. There was a glass door leading to a tiny balcony, too. As promised, Brian could see the lights of Tokyo Tower shimmering in the distance.

Nick showed Brian around. There wasn't much to see beyond the shared bathroom. They hauled Brian's stuff into his bedroom. It barely fit.

"Look, Brian," Nick said at last. "I gotta go check on a story I filed this morning. It shouldn't take too long. Rest up, shower and change, and we'll check out the nightlife."

Alone at last, Brian leaned his surfboard against one wall and plopped down on the bed. The long flight, the harrowing trip from the airport, and the ceaseless banter from his new roommate had taken their toll. Brian soon fell into a deep, fitful sleep.

"Hey, wake up!"

Brian covered his eyes with his hand. No use. He could shut out the light, but Nick Gordon's voice was just too insistent.

"Come on, Shimura!" Nick said, shaking him. "It's ten P.M.—the night is young!"

Brian groaned. He straightened up in the bed and opened his eyes. He looked at his reflection in the mirror. His straight, raven black hair was a mess. There were deep shadows under his eyes. He blinked.

He saw Nick's reflection in the mirror, too. "Jet lag, huh?" Nick asked sympathetically. Brian nodded.

"There's a cure for that," Nick continued. "And it isn't sleeping the night away!"

"Oh?" Brian asked. "Then what *is* the cure?"

"Good food and good friends. Off your meat and on your feet, soldier. It's party time!"

CHAPTER 3

A NIGHT ON THE TOWN

May 12, 1998, 10:45 P.M.
Roppongi-dori Avenue
Tokyo, Japan

Nick and an awestruck Brian navigated the noisy, crowded streets of Roppongi. Brian was amazed at the sheer volume of street life. Even Los Angeles' famed Sunset Strip on a Saturday night lacked the kind of excitement and energy of this district of Tokyo. And it was only Tuesday!

As they walked, Nick chatted while Brian absorbed the exotic sights and sounds. Brian marveled at the sophistication of these Tokyoites. Almost everyone was sporting the most expensive designer clothes from the best European, American, and Japanese houses of fashion. Those who didn't were dressed in wild rock-and-roll regalia. Some sported T-shirts with weird words and phrases in English, Japanese, or French.

A few people were dressed more traditionally. Brian noticed several older women in black kimonos.

The neon lights were amazing. The Tokyo night

was ablaze with brilliant colors. Crazy, busy signs in unreadable *kana* characters flickered and danced. Occasionally a word, phrase, or brand name written in English could be spotted.

Nick explained that Roppongi was the live-music center of Tokyo. As they walked he pointed out various discos and music clubs with exotic names. One club was called Deja vu, another Africa's. A club called the Lexington Queen was surrounded by rockers. The marquee proclaimed, METALLICA—LIVE!

"The hottest meeting spot around here is Amando," Nick told Brian. "We'll check it out later. Let's get something to eat first."

Brian nodded, still scanning the street. Once, when he was fourteen, Brian had visited New York City. But the bright lights of Broadway paled in comparison to the blinding multicolored neon of Roppongi.

Among the throngs that choked the streets, Brian noticed some Americans and Europeans. There were United States Navy and Marine Corps officers and enlisted men—some in dress uniforms, others in civilian clothes, but still recognizable because of their severe haircuts and erect, military posture.

"Why are there so many Westerners here?" Brian asked.

"It's because of the embassies! They're all over the district!" Nick was almost shouting so he could be heard over the blaring music. "And this is *the* hot spot for tourists, too!"

Nick turned a corner and led Brian down yet

another garishly lit, but quieter, street. Brian recognized a familiar sign halfway down the block.

A few minutes later, Brian was sipping a drink with Nick in Tokyo's Hard Rock Cafe. The music was loud, and the place was very crowded. Nick and Brian stood against the wall while they waited for a table.

"Tomorrow you'll meet some of the guys," Nick told Brian. "You have an appointment to meet Boss Gaijin at noon, too."

"Boss Gaijin?" asked Brian.

"Everett P. Endicott the Third. 'Boss Gaijin' to the newsroom. He's—" Nick fell silent as three gorgeous young Japanese women in short skirts and perfect makeup slipped past them, leaving a trail of delightful perfume lingering behind.

Brian cleared his throat. "You were saying?" he said as the three women took seats at the bar and turned their backs to them. Nick, his eyes occasionally straying to the hot young ladies, continued.

"Endicott's the chief of the Tokyo news bureau," Nick said. "He's a dork, plain and simple."

"I gather you don't like him," Brian said.

"I don't think *he* likes *me*. I just had my fourth story in a month rejected tonight."

"I'm sorry," Brian said sympathetically.

"It was a good one, too. Two years ago, a Russian nuclear submarine sank off the coast of Japan, in very deep water—"

"What was a Russian submarine doing there?" Brian interrupted.

"Well, the French were conducting nuclear tests in the South Pacific at the time. And the Chinese had war games, too. The sub was probably observing one or both events—but that ain't the point." Nick took a deep breath.

"The point is that there was a big splash a couple of weeks ago about the deep-sea retrieval research being done by Dr. Ishido in the area where the sub sank. The project is called Sea Base One—"

"Yeah, so?" Brian butted in.

"So Dr. Ishido and his team just packed up and sailed for home today—six months early, with absolutely no explanation. There's a total news blackout!"

"I don't get it," Brian confessed.

"I've been covering the Sea Base One story—as much as Endicott will *let* me cover it, anyway—and let me tell you, something funny is going on." Nick took a breath.

"Three days ago, they reported finding what they thought was the Russian sub's reactor core. Then came the news blackout. Now the whole team is sailing back to Japan—and the whole Sea Base One program is canceled, or postponed, or something!"

Nick looked at Brian. "I got the inside track on this story. Not even Max Hulse, INN's so-called science correspondent, knows what I know." Nick lowered his voice. "They *found* something," he said ominously.

"Like?" Brian asked eagerly.

"*That* I don't know," Nick admitted. "Maybe evidence that the sub was sunk by the Chinese or the French. Maybe radioactive damage of monumental proportions. I really don't know." Nick threw up his hands. Then his eyes narrowed, and he stared off into space.

"But I smell a story," he muttered. "And Everett P. Endicott took me off the assignment." There was bitterness in his voice.

Then he shook his head. "Ah, don't worry about it. We are young, we are free, let's have fun, dinner's on me..."

"It's all right!" They both sang the Supergrass tune in unison, then laughed. The three ladies glanced their way, but Brian and Nick were so busy laughing, they didn't notice.

After that, Nick passed on the latest newsroom gossip. There were new Chinese war games beginning off the coast of Taiwan. Threats of trade sanctions against Japan over an insurance industry dispute. And something else.

"Something big is up," Nick said mysteriously. "I can smell it. Some hot, breaking story is brewing. Something even bigger than Sea Base One."

Brian, whose field of vision had strayed during Nick's news update, tore his eyes away from the three Japanese women. "How do you know it's something big?" he asked.

Nick smiled knowingly. "Endicott was in the conference room with some bigwig field reporters. Nobody would talk to me, which is another sure sign something's up. They never tell us interns anything. We'll learn what's going on when the world does," he concluded.

Then he began telling Brian what kind of work he would be doing for the Independent News Network. This was Nick's second internship to

Japan, so he was something of an expert, at least in his own mind.

"In the first month, you'll be doing boring stuff," Nick informed Brian. "The three Fs, mostly."

"The three Fs?" Brian asked, raising an eyebrow.

"Filing, fact-checking, and finance," Nick replied.

"The first two are obvious, but what's the 'finance' part?" Brian pressed.

"We process the *real* reporters' expense accounts," Nick answered sullenly.

"Oh, well," Brian sighed. "So much for the exciting life of a foreign correspondent."

"I hope you didn't go into journalism for excitement," Nick said.

"Not really," Brian answered honestly. "I was never much interested in that kind of excitement."

"Are you a current affairs junkie? Politics, stuff like that?" Nick continued. "You don't look the type."

"No way!" Brian laughed. "Actually, I want to be a sportscaster someday. Think about it. Super Bowl and World Series tickets for life!"

"I have a confession to make," Nick said solemnly. "I am a *nerd*. Sports never interested me much."

"Well," Brian continued, the disappointment evident in his voice, "my original internship was to cover the Winter Olympics in Nagano, but…"

"But they were held four months ago." Nick finished Brian's thought. "I've been to the Japanese Alps—they're really beautiful. Great skiing!" Nick paused. "It's too bad you missed it," he added.

"Yeah, well. I had to postpone my internship. There was…a family emergency," Brian replied. He didn't elaborate. He didn't want to tell Nick the whole story just yet. *Maybe I don't want to see another look of pity in a friend's eyes,* Brian mused. In any case, now was not the time for "the whole story."

Nick's eyes drifted to the three Japanese women. They were drinking exotic cocktails and giggling among themselves.

"Well," he said, still gazing at the girls. "Since you missed the Olympics, why come to Japan *now*?"

"Gee, round-eyes...I Japanese-American," Brian teased.

Nick turned up his nose. "As a full-blooded WASP, I never went in for that hyphenated-American stuff. Enlighten me."

"Well," said Brian. "According to my dad, it was time for me to make that voyage of discovery. Find my roots, you know. My father was born here in Tokyo, and I have family here."

"Family...hmmm. Any cousins—*female* cousins?" Nick asked slyly.

Brian laughed. "Nah, only my Uncle Maxwell."

"Uncle *Maxwell*?" Nick replied. "That's an odd name for a Japanese man."

"He isn't Japanese," Brian said. "Uncle Maxwell is an officer in the U.S. Navy. He met my aunt—my dad's sister—when he was stationed here during the Korean War. They got married...my aunt died about five years ago, but Uncle Maxwell still lives in Japan. He's still in the Navy, too."

"Interesting," Nick said, his eyes straying to the Japanese girls at the bar. "So, you were saying, your dad wanted you to intern here?"

"He was a kid when he left Japan," Brian continued. "My dad met my mother in California, they got married, and he never came back. But he talked about Japan a lot when I was growing up. So when this second Japanese internship came down, I grabbed it."

"But you don't speak much Japanese," Nick observed.

"No," Brian confessed. "My mother wouldn't let us speak Japanese in the house. She said that was part of the Old World, a world she didn't want to go back to. My mom had a career, friends. She liked being an American. She was as American as apple pie, or so my dad used to say."

Maybe it was the noise, or the women across the bar, or by choice—but Nick didn't catch the past tense Brian used when he spoke of his mother.

"My father likes to talk about Japan like it's some paradise," Brian continued. "I figured I had to see it."

"So why did he leave Japan, if he loved it here so much?" Nick asked.

Brian shrugged and was silent. It occurred to him that he never thought to ask his father that question. Not that his dad would have given him a straight answer, anyway. Dr. Ryuhei Shimura was the strong, silent type. John Wayne by way of Toshiro Mifune.

"So," Brian said, changing the subject. "Why are *you* here?"

"Not many news agencies offer science correspondent internships. INN does, and it's here in Japan," Nick answered.

"I'd never peg you for the scientific type," Brian said.

"I wanted to be a scientist, but I'm not good at math," Nick admitted frankly. "I can sure talk the lingo, though, and that's all a good science correspondent has to do!"

"Oh, it's *that* easy," Brian said dubiously.

"Hey, Mister He-shoots-he-scores, allow me to demonstrate."

Then Nick launched into a live, on-the-spot science report of the activities of the group of chic Japanese women they'd been scoping out since they'd arrived. "As you can see, those females are well-adapted to their environment. Their bright plumage attracts members of the opposite sex."

Brian watched as a Japanese salaryman—office worker—tried to engage the prettiest girl in conversation. Brian noticed that another man was circling the women.

"But nature can be capricious," Nick continued in a serious tone. "The bright plumage that attracts potential mates also attracts predators from other territories."

Unfortunately for the Japanese man, a tall, muscular U.S. Marine was also trying to talk up the women.

"It becomes a question of survival," Nick intoned. "Can the male of this species protect his potential reproductive partners against the predatory behavior of other wild beasts?"

Just then, the girl turned her back on the man in uniform. She reached out and took the salaryman by the arm. He led her to a table in the crowded dining area.

"In this case, the predator was driven back," Nick said. "Or, as my esteemed colleague would say…"

"He shoots, he scores," Brian said. They both laughed. At that moment, the hostess tapped Nick on the shoulder and they followed her to a table.

Brian found he enjoyed Nick Gordon's company. By the end of the evening, Brian realized that Nick knew a lot about him, but Brian still knew little about his roommate. It really didn't matter, though. Nick was funny, straightforward, sincere, and easy to talk to.

Brian knew he'd made a friend. A *good* friend.

CHAPTER 4

THE OCEAN BOILS!

May 12, 1998, 11:47 P.M.
East China Sea

With powerful binoculars, Captain Koh scanned the dark ocean that surrounded his ship—a Korean commercial vessel bound for Los Angeles. The East China Sea was calm, the night still. The dark mantle of sky twinkled with the lights from a thousand stars. It could not be clearer. The weather could not be more fair.

But Koh was edgy. His nerves tingled and he could not relax. That he could find no reason for his agitation only made it worse. After sixty years of seagoing experience, Koh's instincts were seldom wrong.

Koh crossed the dimly lit bridge of the *Azure Dragon* and scanned the ocean on the opposite side.

Nothing.

Koh shivered, though the night was balmy. "Perhaps some tea," he said aloud.

"Pardon me, Captain?" asked the young ensign who manned the wheel.

"It is nothing, Rhee," Captain Koh replied. "I only wished for some hot tea."

"I'll call the galley," Ensign Rhee said, reaching for the horn. While the ensign spoke, Koh brought the binoculars back up to his eyes and scanned the horizon once again.

Old habits die hard, Koh thought. *I should remember that I am a civilian now—that I command a freighter, not a fast attack boat.*

"The tea will be here momentarily," Ensign Rhee said, interrupting his commander's thoughts.

"Thank you," Koh replied. He continued to scan the horizon.

"Are we on course?" Koh asked after a moment.

"On course, and ahead of schedule," Rhee barked back proudly. Despite his misgivings, Koh smiled. Rhee was a conscientious officer, and Koh enjoyed commanding such men. *It's a shame that Ensign Rhee did not pursue a career in the Republic of Korea's Navy,* he mused.

The steel door opened and the galley mate entered the bridge. He was a short, squat man—a former factory worker from Inchon. The galley mate smelled of kimchee, the powerful pickled cabbage the sailors of the *Azure Dragon* ate on a daily basis.

"Tea, sir?" the fat man asked.

Koh nodded. "Pour some for Rhee, too," the captain said. Soon the two officers were sipping steaming mugs of strong green tea.

"The weather is fair," Rhee said, his spirits high. "It is a good omen! Perhaps we will finish our route early."

Koh was silent. Rhee rattled on nervously. "It would be good to get back to Seoul before Independence Day."

August 12 was South Korea's Liberation, or Independence, Day—the biggest holiday of the year, next to Chusok, Korea's version of Thanksgiving. Independence Day commemorated the day in 1945 when the Japanese occupation of Korea ended and the nation was reborn. Koh did some mental calculations.

"I do not think our three-month schedule will rob you of the pleasure of Seoul's parades," Koh said dryly. "Or its women."

"It is not that," Rhee said hesitantly. "It's my wife. She is due to give birth to our first child around that time."

"Ahhh," Koh said, nodding. "A child born on Liberation Day. That *is* a good omen. I toast your unborn child, Ensign Rhee."

The two men clinked mugs and drank. Rhee beamed with pride. For the first time that night, Captain Koh relaxed.

I'm getting old, he thought. *My instincts are not as sharp as they were. It seems that tea was all I needed.*

Koh stifled a yawn, and glanced at the ship's clock.

But suddenly, out of the corner of his eye, Koh caught a flash of light. Ensign Rhee grunted. He saw it, too—off the starboard bow.

There it was again. "It looks like lightning," Rhee said. But Koh was not so sure. He had never seen lightning that came from under *the ocean itself!*

Again! This time Captain Koh was sure of it.

He heard voices from the deck. Others had seen the eerie blue lights. The horn squawked. Ensign Rhee answered.

"Bridge," he said, his eyes never leaving the starboard horizon.

"It's Tae, on watch, sir." Rhee could hear the fear and uncertainty in the voice that came over the microphone. "There's something strange to starboard."

"Yes," Rhee replied. "We see it. Stand by."

Captain Koh searched the area where he last spotted the blue light. Even through his binoculars, he could see no other ship. *Perhaps it's some natural phenomenon,* Koh mused, though he knew otherwise. With a start, Koh realized his instincts had been right!

"Ensign," he barked. "Contact headquarters!"

Rhee grabbed the radiophone and began speaking. Koh watched the horizon tensely. *There!* Koh practically cried out. Another flash of light—and this one much closer.

Suddenly, the ocean underneath the ship seemed to catch fire. Blue light surrounded the *Azure Dragon*, bathing the ship in an eerie glow. Captain Koh opened the door to the bridge and stepped out onto the walkway. He heard voices. Members of the crew were rushing on deck to see the strange lights. Even Ensign Rhee strained to see the display of eerie lights, though he never let go of the wheel.

The wide patch of ocean surrounding the *Azure Dragon* was luminescent. It was a strange, unearthly spectacle. *But not without beauty,* Koh thought philosophically as he leaned over the railing to get a better look.

The glowing lights seemed to come from far under the water. This display of unearthly brilliance was like nothing Koh had ever seen or heard about. As the seconds ticked by, the radiance grew in intensity.

"Captain, look!" Seaman Tae shouted from the deck above. He was pointing down at the churning ocean. Koh looked down. The light was now so intense that it was difficult to stare directly into it. Koh blinked—his eyes were watering. Squinting against the glare, Koh examined the water that lapped against the hull.

Finally, he noticed that dark objects were floating up from under the surface of the bubbling ocean. The shapes were silhouetted in the blue brilliance.

Fish!

Hundreds of them. *Thousands* of them. Fish of all sizes and shapes. And they were all dead.

Koh clutched the railing. His mind reeled. And then he felt a moist heat against his exposed skin. Koh sniffed a strange odor. A rich, salty, briny smell, not unlike fish soup.

"The ocean!" Koh screamed as the realization hit him. "It's boiling!"

Koh turned to Ensign Rhee. "Full speed ahead," he cried. "Get the ship out of here!"

Rhee grabbed the throttle and pushed forward. The engines coughed, then sputtered. Then died. Rhee grabbed the horn. "Engine room!" he screamed. "ENGINE ROOM!"

Just then, fire alarms went off all over the ship.

As the klaxons blared, the sailors and officers of the *Azure Dragon* rushed to their emergency fire stations.

Captain Koh ran back onto the bridge. "Have you made contact with headquarters yet?" he demanded.

"Yes, sir!" Rhee replied. "They are standing by."

Captain Koh grabbed the radiophone. "Mayday, mayday," he called. "This is Captain Koh of the *Azure Dragon,* requesting assistance. We have a fire aboard. Our location is—"

At that second, a muffled explosion rocked the ship. The whole vessel shuddered once. Then the lights faded.

For a tense moment, the bridge went dark. Then the battery-powered emergency lights came up. In the dull illumination, Koh could see the fear on Ensign Rhee's face.

Suddenly, the ship was rocked by a thousand lesser explosions. The noise sounded like thousands of firecrackers going off. Rhee grabbed the horn. "What is happening?" he cried in panic.

"Sir," an unidentified voice said over the speaker. "It's the cargo hold. There is heat, and fire—" Then the speaker went dead.

Of course! Koh understood at last. That sound came from the containers stacked in the ship's cargo hold, where thousands of Korean-made televisions being exported to the Americas were stored.

The heat below the hull must be tremendous, Captain Koh realized. The explosions were the sound of thousands of cathode ray tubes bursting apart.

Seaman Tae rushed onto the bridge. His clothes were scorched and he smelled of smoke. "Captain," he gasped. "There is something...something horrible! It's outside!"

"Make sense, sailor!" Rhee shouted.

At that second, a rolling, bell-like, feral roar slammed against their eardrums. The clamor reverberated through the entire ship. Koh covered his ears. Tae cowered in the corner, his arms covering his head.

The terrible sound emanated from the ocean underneath the *Azure Dragon*'s decks. Then the cacophony slowly faded and died. The ocean around the ship churned and bubbled more violently.

Someone on deck screamed.

While Koh watched, a dark mass the size of a mountain rose up from the ocean alongside the freighter. Its tremendous motion rocked the ship, and the awesome vision stunned the onlookers of the *Azure Dragon*.

Koh's mouth dropped open as he stared at the apparition before him. Ensign Rhee screamed in shock and fear. He clutched the ship's wheel as if it were his only link to sanity.

Now I understand, Koh thought.

With the calmness that comes with the knowledge that death is imminent, Koh lifted the radiophone and spoke.

"Headquarters, this is *Azure Dragon*," he said. "We are under attack...by the monster Godzilla."

The mountain of flesh and bone that stood before them roared again. The sound split eardrums as it echoed throughout the hollow steel shell of the *Azure Dragon*.

Koh turned to Ensign Rhee. The young man's face was pale and sweaty. As he clutched the wheel with white knuckles, his mouth twitched and moved. But no sound came out.

Koh, taking pity on this young man, reached out and touched Ensign Rhee's arm. Slowly, mechanically, Rhee's head turned and he faced his captain with unseeing eyes.

At that moment, a blast of blue fire rained down upon the *Azure Dragon*. The powerful, burning energy blasted right through the windows of the bridge, showering the occupants with droplets of molten glass.

A nanosecond later, Koh felt the terrible heat.

He watched in horror as the flesh bubbled and melted off Ensign Rhee's face. He heard Seaman Tae screaming, but the sound seemed far away. Then Koh felt a burning sensation. He looked down at his own body.

My clothes are on fire, he realized numbly. Then his flesh began to melt, too.

Finally, mercifully, the thousands of gallons of flammable diesel fuel that fed the ship's huge engines erupted into a fireball.

The *Azure Dragon* was blown to bits.

CHAPTER 5

THE GOOD, THE BAD, AND THE PORTLY

May 13, 1998, 11:58 A.M.
The newsroom, INN headquarters
Tokyo, Japan

All dressed up like a Thanksgiving turkey.

That's exactly how Brian Shimura felt as he stepped out of the elevator and onto the twentieth floor, where INN's suite of executive offices were located. He took another deep breath as the doors closed behind him. Brian found himself alone in a tastefully decorated waiting area.

The day had not begun auspiciously.

Nick woke him up in time for a quick shower and shave. Then Brian, clad in his best suit, waited for half an hour, until Nick finished dressing. Brian was stunned when his roommate emerged from his bedroom in blue jeans, a faded shirt, and a blue blazer with matching tie. "Don't worry, Brian, things are pretty relaxed once you've made an impression," Nick informed him.

Then Nick led Brian to the staff cafeteria, where he gobbled up a hearty meal. Brian, his stomach in knots, fingered his fruit salad.

"Nervous about meeting Boss Gaijin?" Nick asked.

"A little," Brian confessed.

Nick nodded sagely. "Just remember that Superman has his Perry White, Spider-Man has his J. Jonah Jameson, and we've got Everett P. Endicott the Turd—er, Third!" Nick said. "My advice to you is the same I offer to every other rookie who's wet behind the ears! Suck up, defer to Endicott's infinite wisdom, and don't talk back. Do all of those things, and you'll be just fine."

Brian shook his head dubiously.

"Look, there's really not much the guy can do to you," Nick said. "The worst he can dish out is a week in the mailroom, then a stint as a factchecker…and he won't do that to an up-front guy like yourself!" Nick slapped him on the back. "You're in like Flynn, my man."

After breakfast, Nick led Brian to the personnel office and dumped him there.

"I'll meet you in the newsroom at eleven-thirty," Nick promised. "You *might* be done with your paperwork by then. Have fun!"

Nick trotted off just as a smiling Japanese woman handed Brian a huge folder. "Please fill these out, and I will bring you the rest," she said.

Two and a half hours later, Brian found the newsroom. The room itself was a maze of cubicles. Most of the desks had computer stations tied to a central information bank. There were dozens of men and woman busily processing bits of information. These items would be used as fodder for INN's hundreds of radio and television outlets worldwide.

A leather-faced Japanese man wearing a white shirt and a stained tie touched Brian's shoulder. He pointed to a cubicle in the far corner. "Sit there!" he said, then hurried off.

Brian sat down in front of a desk, a computer terminal, and a telephone. Otherwise, the cubicle was barren. Brian eyed the beige plastic partitions warily. His claustrophobia mounted.

"Knock, knock!" Nick announced, peeking around the edge of the partition.

"Hey," Brian said with a wave of his hand.

"Almost time to meet Boss Gaijin, eh?" Nick asked.

"I'm afraid I'm gonna call him Boss Gaijin instead of Mr. Endicott," Brian said weakly.

"Don't worry so much!" Nick replied. "You're here now. He can't send you back home. You'll be fine."

Brian nodded. Nick was trying to comfort him, but his words had the opposite effect. "Hey, I have to talk to Boss Gaijin—I mean, Mr. Endicott—too. But you better meet him first—seeing me always puts him in a foul mood."

Just then the phone buzzed. Brian lifted the receiver. "Mr. Endicott will see you now," a woman's voice said on the other end of the line.

Brian rose, took a deep breath, and turned to Nick. "Wish me luck," he said.

Nick smiled as he straightened Brian's tie. "Break a leg," Nick said. "Preferably *his*." They headed to the bank of elevators together. Nick waited with Brian.

"I'm going to find Yoshi," Nick announced. "He's the best cameraman in Tokyo, and a great guy, too.

You'll love him! Maybe I can wrangle us up an assignment."

The elevator arrived and Brian stepped inside. He pushed the button for the twentieth floor and rode up.

As he left the elevator, a young woman in a well-tailored designer jacket and a *very* short skirt turned the corner. She brushed her long auburn hair away from her face and smiled.

"You're Brian?" she asked. He nodded.

"A pleasure to meet you," she said brightly, extending her hand. "I'm May McGovern, Mr. Endicott's personal assistant."

"Hi," Brian said, momentarily tongue-tied. *She's gorgeous!* he thought.

"Mr. Endicott will be with you shortly," Ms. McGovern said. "If you'll just follow me."

She led him down a long hallway lined with office doors made of rich wood. They were all closed. As they walked, Brian eagerly anticipated the rest of his first day on the job in his mind.

"Here we are, Mr. Shimura," May McGovern said as she opened a door, then ushered him into a huge corner office. With a final smile, May closed the door behind him. Brian turned.

In the center of the room, between two huge windows that looked out over Tokyo, sat a massive teak desk. Behind the desk was a huge chair, and on that chair sat Everett P. Endicott. He did not look up from the papers spread out all over his desk.

"Find your office okay, Shimura?" he asked, still reading the papers in front of him.

"Yes, sir," Brian replied. *You mean my cubicle,* he thought.

"Good," Endicott nodded absently. "Sit down."

Brian reached out to shake Everett Endicott's hand, but the man's eyes never left the papers in front of him. After a moment, Brian lowered his hand and sat down.

"You were supposed to be here for the Winter Olympics in Nagano," Endicott said with a trace of annoyance in his voice. "I could have used another sportscaster wannabe back then. I don't have much use for one now."

"Yes, well, I'm sorry," Brian answered uncomfortably. "It was...unavoidable." He didn't want to explain yet again about the family tragedy that had held up his arrival for four months.

"Never mind," Endicott said, glancing at the papers again. Brian realized with a start that his new boss was reading his academic file. *Well,* Brian thought, *he already knows why I wasn't here, then.*

They sat in silence for a minute or two. Finally, Endicott lifted his beady eyes and stared at Brian.

Everett P. Endicott the Third was a portly man, though his tailored suit hid some of the damage. The suit was the best money could buy, which was about what Brian expected of the grandson of the owner and founder of INN, but there was no hiding the thick roll of fat under his chin, nor the puffy hands that sat crossed on the desk.

Brian realized he was staring, and his vision drifted to the view outside the windows. Tokyo at lunchtime.

"I don't know what you'll do or where you'll work right now," Endicott said. "Not much interest in Japanese baseball in the States. You won't be doing work in your chosen area of interest. I'm sorry for that.

"So, for the present, I'm going to assign you to the mailroom. In a week or so we'll see about moving you up to filing and fact checking."

Brian groaned inside, but carefully hid his disappointment.

Endicott nodded, obviously happy with his own solution. "Yes, that *will* do…"

Then the big man rose ponderously from his desk. He stuck out his beefy hand and took Brian's.

"Welcome aboard," he said. "I'll have my secretary draw up your assignment roster. See May if you have any problems at all."

Just then, the office door flew open. May McGovern tried to block the door, but Nick Gordon pushed right past her. She stared at his back, her eyes ablaze.

"Sorry to barge in, chief, but *this* is important!" Nick announced.

Endicott's face clouded. He motioned May to return to the outer office. Then Endicott focused his gaze on Nick.

"Hello, Gordon," he said icily. "To what do I owe the pleasure of your company?"

"Well, you know that the Kawasaki plant is opening its new, totally robotic assembly line tomorrow. There's a big bash tonight, a tour—"

"And?" Endicott interrupted coldly.

"Well, if you sign our vouchers, Brian and I can

take the bullet train. We can be there in a couple of hours. We'll take Yoshi and his camera, too. We'll stay the night, then cover the event tomorrow. I can show Brian here the ropes, and it'll be a great story for *INN Science Sunday*."

"*I'll* be the judge of what's a great story," Endicott barked pompously.

"Well, chief," Nick said innocently. "If you'd rather, I'll work with Max Hulse. Isn't he covering that Sea Base One story?"

"What's your assignment for the week, Gordon?" Endicott demanded.

"Fact-checking," Nick said with a sigh.

"Then *do it!*" Endicott shot back. "Anyway, I've already sent Blackthorn Adams to cover the Kawasaki story. So get out of here, and take your new roommate with you!"

Brian grabbed Nick's arm and pulled him out of the office. Nick left without a struggle.

"What a jerk!" Nick declared as the office door shut behind them.

"What happened to your advice?" Brian asked. "Especially the part about sucking up…and *shutting* up?"

"No, no." Nick shook his head. "That's what *you're* supposed to do—"

"You little sneak!" May McGovern cried angrily. Startled, Nick and Brian turned to face her. May's hands were on her hips and her green eyes were flashing.

"I *told* you before, Nick Gordon," she hissed, wagging a finger at him. "Never *ever* barge in on the boss! Do you want to see me *fired?*"

She slammed some files down on her desk. Papers scattered. "Knowing *you*, that's probably exactly what you want!" she spat.

Nick stammered. Brian blushed. When May realized no answer—or apology—was forthcoming, she pointed to the door. "Get out of here, Gordon," she commanded.

Nick and Brian rushed to the elevators and returned to the newsroom.

Back at Endicott's office, May apologized to her boss. "Don't worry about it, May," the fat man said as he settled into his chair.

"It was all that moron Gordon's fault," May said. She was still hissing mad. "I can't wait until INN sends him back to Cleveland!"

A few minutes after she returned to her desk and gathered up her files, the intercom buzzed.

"Get Blackthorn Adams on the line," Endicott told her. "I want him to go up to Kawasaki's new plant and cover the opening of their robotic assembly line. He can take that new cameraman, what's his name?"

"Yoshi Masahara," May answered.

"Yeah, that's him," Endicott replied. "Tell them to tape a feature for *INN Science Sunday*. They should go up there tonight on the bullet train. I'll sign their vouchers."

At two o'clock, Nick stopped by Brian's cubicle. Brian noticed his roommate was still in a foul mood.

"All right, I admit it," Nick confessed. "The whole

Kawasaki thing was just a scam...I *really* wanted him to assign me to the Sea Base One story." Nick sighed. "He probably didn't even *know* about the Kawasaki plant opening!"

Brian yawned and stretched. "Well, I'm glad I didn't have to rush out of Tokyo tonight," he said. "I could use another night on the town." Brian remembered the three women in the Hard Rock Cafe from the night before.

"What *really* bugs me," Nick said, oblivious to Brian's hint, "is that Max Hulse gets to cover Sea Base! *Max Hulse!* The most boring newsman on the planet. Do you know what they call him around here? I'll tell you. *Lacks Pulse!*"

Brian suspected that *they* really just meant *Nick*. He was getting to know his roommate pretty well.

A little while later, in the middle of a conversation about the nightclubs in Tokyo, Nick's eyes widened. He waved his hand and shouted across the newsroom.

"Hey, Yoshi!" Nick cried. "Over here."

Brian saw a young Japanese man in a blue suit, speaking with the grizzled Japanese man who had first showed him his cubicle. The younger man turned, smiled, and waved back at Nick. He finished his business with the older man and then sauntered over.

"Brian Shimura," Nick said, "this is the best cameraman in Tokyo—Yoshi Masahara!"

"Welcome to Japan," Yoshi said with a slight bow. Then he extended his hand.

"Call me Brian," the American replied.

"And you, please call me Yoshi!" the Japanese

man replied. His English was excellent. He only slightly slurred the *l* in *please.*

"I was just convincing our young friend here that a night on the town would do him good!" Nick said to Yoshi. "I hope you can join us tonight."

A frown appeared on Yoshi's face. "So sorry," he said apologetically. "Just got an assignment from Takao-san...I must go with Blackthorn Adams on bullet train. I leave tonight."

"Are you covering the Kawasaki plant opening?" Nick said suspiciously.

"Yes!" Yoshi replied. "Last-minute assignment."

Nick threw up his arms and screamed. "That rotten little—" Nick bit back his curse and, without another word, stormed off toward the elevators.

"He does that often," Yoshi said to Brian. "Excuse me for asking an impolite question."

"Of course," Brian said.

"Is this...an *American* thing?" Yoshi asked.

"No," Brian replied. "I think it's a *Nick Gordon* thing."

"Hai!" said Yoshi. "I thought so."

CHAPTER 6

S.O.S. FROM THE SEA OF JAPAN

May 29, 1998, 6:23 A.M.
The gate to the Pusan ferry
Hakata, Japan

Kim Park liked riding the bullet train okay, but he *loved* to ride the Pusan ferry. The trip on the ultra-modern train was nowhere near as magical as the 150-mile ferryboat ride between Korea and northern Japan, where he and his mother and father now lived.

Unfortunately, his mother hated it. Kim, only nine years old, couldn't figure out why. He loved riding a boat, *any* kind of boat. And he loved the sea.

"Kim!" his mother called from a bench as far from the water as she could get. "Come down from that railing before you fall in!"

Kim took one last look over the fence at the gray water lapping against the pier. Then he turned, jumped down, and ran back to his mother.

"How long before the ferry sails?" Kim asked.

"We can get on board very soon," she answered

nervously. Kim looked at the boat. *Yes,* he thought, his excitement mounting. *People are already lining up!*

"Come on, Mother," Kim said, pulling her arm. "Let's get in line so we can get a good seat." Reluctantly, she rose and gathered up her bags. Kim helped her.

"Will Uncle Pak be waiting for us on the other side?" Kim asked as they approached the ship.

"Uncle Pak, and his wife, Hyon, and even Uncle Cho—everyone is coming for your aunt's wedding tomorrow," his mother said with a smile.

Kim knew his mother was excited about this trip. Things were better for Kim's family now that Dad had started working for a Japanese company, but Kim knew his mother missed her friends and family back in Korea. Kim missed his little cousins, too, but he *really* missed Uncle Pak, a colonel in the Army of the Republic of Korea.

Uncle Pak was Kim's hero.

Kim skipped as they approached the ferry. The Pusan ferryboat was an old vessel—nearly half a century old, in fact. Despite a relatively fresh coat of nondescript gray paint, the ship showed her age. But not to Kim. In his imagination, it was the fiercest fighting ship on the ocean—and he was the captain.

As cars and trucks filled the ferry's hull, Kim and his mother climbed up onto the upper deck. Kim climbed the steps effortlessly, but his mother was breathing heavily by the time they had reached the top. Kim knew she had not slept on the bullet train, though he had.

The ferry was only half full. But it was still early—in another hour or so, the pier would be filled with people heading across the Sea of Japan for work.

Kim was disappointed that his mother chose to sit inside the passenger cabin instead of out on the deck. She said she was cold, but Kim knew that his mother was afraid of the ocean. He did not argue.

From his seat, Kim scanned the other passengers. There were men in suits and work clothes, and women, too. There were truck drivers, and even a small group of Korean nuns. For a moment, Kim's gaze lingered on a young Caucasian man and a Korean girl. They were holding hands.

Finally, the whistle blew, and the engine began to throb. Kim could feel the deck vibrate. He watched as men untied the thick ropes that moored the ship to the dock. The ferry pulled slowly away from the pier and out to sea. Soon she was steaming toward Korea.

Will Adams rubbed his tired eyes. *What am I doing on the Pusan ferry—on my way to South Korea—at six-thirty in the morning?* he asked himself for the hundredth time. And, for the hundredth time, he found the answer to his question.

Because I'm with Soonji.

Will shook his head and ran his fingers through his fashionably short hair and goatee. *Face it, buddy, you're hooked. You'd go to the ends of the earth if she asked you!*

Will Adams had met Soonji Hwan-Duk three days ago while he was visiting Hakusan National

Park with several friends from the American School. In the spring, the national parks of northern Honshu, Japan's main island, are a bustling tourist attraction. Will liked hiking, and Honshu had some of the best trails.

On one of them, he met Soonji and her friends. Since then, the two of them had been inseparable. Fortunately for them both, they were on vacation.

Will had just graduated from high school and would be heading back to America—and to Harvard—in the fall. Until then, he was spending a couple of months with his divorced father. Blackthorn Adams, Will's dad, was one of the science correspondents for INN. Soonji seemed very impressed by that.

For Soonji, "vacation" was a permanent condition. Her father was a prominent politician in the current regime in Seoul. She had time—and money—to spare. At her insistence, Will had parted with his friends and followed her to Hakata. While they were in the city, they visited the museum and some Buddhist temples.

Will wasn't much interested in temples, but he *was* interested in Soonji.

"Wake up, sleepyhead," Soonji chided him, pouting. "Don't be tiresome. Talk to me!"

"Sorry," Will said, shaking himself awake. He longed for a cup of hot coffee. He looked longingly at her, too, as she took his hand and gripped it.

"Soon you'll see my homeland. It's much more beautifuller than Japan," she insisted.

Will smiled. He found her malapropisms cute. In fact, he found everything about her cute. Will wasn't blind to Soonji's faults. He knew she seemed like a shallow teenage girl who was moody, self-centered, and spoiled rotten. But he also knew that she was very beautiful, and that, for the moment, he was hooked.

"Finally the lazy sailors to get their stupid butts moving at last!" Soonji muttered impatiently in butchered English as the ferry pulled away from the pier.

The waters were calm, but the route was foggy as the Pusan ferry chugged its way toward the Korean peninsula.

On the ancient ship's bridge, high atop the upper decks, the captain scanned the waters ahead. The ferry was already over an hour into its journey, and the Sea of Japan had remained calm. The visibility, however, was less than adequate. The rising sun had not yet burned away the fog. It was an unnatural fog that seemed to envelop the sea in eerie patches. The ferry had been sailing into and out of these huge banks all morning.

"I can see more fog ahead," the captain announced. He lowered the binoculars from his weatherbeaten face and turned to the man clutching the wheel.

"Keep the collision radar running, but do not slow down," he commanded.

The other man nodded, but was not happy with his captain's decision. The so-called "collision radar" on this old tub didn't always detect objects in the water ahead, especially objects that were low in the water.

But I'm not the captain, the man thought bitterly.

As ordered, the wheelman pushed the throttle forward and the ferry sliced through the waves at a faster rate.

Less than a mile ahead of the ferry, sea birds roosted among strange, rocky outcroppings that projected from the water at odd angles in three long rows. The pointed tips of these outcroppings, which were stained dirty white with bird droppings, rose over fifty feet above the waves.

Kim, standing on the bow, spotted the three rows of rocks. He squinted against the wind and leaned over the rail to get a better look. He had made this trip twice, but had never noticed this strange rock formation before.

He heard a sound. The passenger cabin door opened, and then closed, behind him. Some passengers had come out of the warmth of the interior and onto the windswept deck.

Kim turned.

It was the American student and his girlfriend, the pretty Korean girl. Kim knew that the boy was an American—he'd heard him speak English.

Relieved that it was not his mother come to fetch him, Kim returned his gaze to the rocky formation.

That's strange, Kim thought. *The rocks seem to have moved.* The formation had slipped into a fog bank, and then emerged again—this time it seemed much closer to the ferry.

Kim heard a startled exclamation behind him.

The couple had spotted the bird-covered rocks, too. The teenaged boy began jabbering in English.

On the bridge of the Pusan ferry, the captain and the wheelman heard the collision alarm go off.

"All stop!" the captain shouted, even before he saw the object in the ferry's path.

As the wheelman pulled back on the throttles, the captain lifted his binoculars and scanned the waters ahead.

At first he saw nothing. Rolling fog obscured his vision. Then the mist seemed to part and the captain spotted the floating mass of bony spikes. The three rows of objects were towering out of the water and drifting into the ferry's path.

"What is it?" the captain asked the wheelman. But the man at the throttle was far too busy trying to halt the forward momentum of the ship to answer his commanding officer. With a sinking feeling in the pit of his stomach, the ferry captain returned his gaze to the horizon. He watched helplessly as the object drifted closer and closer to his ship.

In desperation, the captain reached for the steam whistle and pulled the chain. The loud blast cut through the fog. Birds, which had been roosting on the floating rocks, took to the air in a flurry of wings.

"Reverse all engines!" the captain cried, his eyes locked on the barrier on the horizon.

"Full reverse!" the wheelman answered, throwing the throttle in the opposite direction.

The engines groaned in protest as the propellers under the stern reversed direction. The whole ship shuddered. The captain and wheelman were thrown forward by the momentum of the vessel. Then the ship seemed to stop.

Before it could move backward, however, the Pusan ferry slammed into the floating mass with a sickening sound of grinding metal.

On the bridge, the captain and wheelman were knocked off their feet. The captain landed hard on the deck. The wheel itself was pulled out of the wheelman's grip as it twisted to the side. Indeed, the whole ferry was pushed to the side. Then its bow was lifted into the air.

"Damage report!" the captain screamed into the radio. "I want a damage report!"

"Captain!" an excited voice cried over the intercom. "The hull has been breached. We are taking on water."

"Damn," the captain cursed. He immediately reached for the long-range radio.

The captain keyed the mike. "This is the Pusan ferry," he said urgently. "Mayday…mayday. We have collided with an object and are taking on water… Mayday! Mayday!"

Will Adams managed to push Soonji and the little Korean boy back inside the passenger compartment right before the collision. Like everyone else, they were knocked off their feet. Now all of the ferry passengers were in a panic. Most of them were screaming in fear.

When the ship finally seemed to settle, the passengers calmed down a bit.

Will held Soonji down as he rose unsteadily to

his feet. "Stay there," he said. Pale with fright, Soonji could only nod.

As Will cautiously approached the windows, people inside the ferry were still talking excitedly. One woman's panic-filled voice cut through the noise. "Kim! Kim!" she cried frantically.

Kim turned when he heard his mother calling him. He rushed across the heaving deck to her side.

"Mom!" he cried. "We hit some rocks. *Floating* rocks! I saw them moving!"

Kim's mother ignored his words. She pulled her son close and held him. The whole ship vibrated as the engine strained to move the ferry. The ship seemed to be stuck, as if it had run aground.

Just then, several crewmen ran into the cabin. They began taking down inflatable life rafts that were stored in the cabin's ceiling. One of them produced a bullhorn.

"We must abandon ship," the sailor said through the loudspeaker. "The hull has been ruptured and we are taking on water. Please remain calm. Emergency calls have already been sent. Help is on the way. As a precaution, we will now board the lifeboats in an orderly fashion. Please remain calm."

Of course, his words had the opposite effect. The passengers were thrown into a panic once again. Women sobbed. Men cried out. Some of the crowd tried to take the inflatable rafts away from the sailors. Fights broke out.

Though Will Adams knew almost no Korean, he understood the pandemonium all around him. *This ship is sinking!* He glanced down at Soonji. Her face was white with panic. She clung to the deck as if it were a lifeline.

A sinking lifeline, Will thought glumly.

Nearby, Kim's mother clutched her son close. She could imagine no more horrible fate than drowning. It had been her lifelong fear. But she did not worry for herself—she prayed only for her young son's life.

Meanwhile, the young American stood up and looked out of the cabin window, toward the bow of the ship.

Suddenly, he gasped and took several steps back.

Kim, his mother, and a few others turned when they heard Will cry out. They, too gasped as a dark shadow rose up and fell across the bow of the Pusan ferry.

As the frightened, unbelieving passengers and crew watched in awe and horror, a giant monster rose up out of the Sea of Japan with an ear-shattering roar!

CHAPTER 7

GOJIRA!

May 29, 1998, 7:18 A.M.
The Pusan ferry
Sea of Japan

"It's *Gojira!*" one of the sailors screamed. All eyes turned to the large windows.

The sailor let go of the uninflated raft he held and it dropped to the deck. The sailor hit the deck, too, and curled up in a quivering mass of fear. A nearby passenger—a burly man—quickly snatched up the raft and pushed for the exit. Another man grabbed the raft out of *his* hands, and a fight broke out.

In seconds, the Pusan ferry erupted in pandemonium. One woman screamed and fainted. She hit the deck hard because everyone else was too startled by the appearance of the now-legendary monster to catch her. Other women, and many men, too, began to scream. Children sobbed in fear.

Will Adams looked up as the shadow fell over him.

Godzilla! he thought, taking two steps backward. He stared awestruck at the apparition standing before him. *Gojira*—the Japanese name for the prehistoric monster known worldwide as Godzilla—was supposed to be dead.

Hell, Will thought, *Godzilla never should have existed in the first place!*

As Will stared at the creature, panic swept through the rest of the passengers. All semblance of order was gone. People rushed for the exits, thinking they could escape the creature by jumping into the Sea of Japan. Will stifled his own panic and observed this incredible freak of nature with a critical, objective eye that would do his reporter father proud.

Godzilla looked like a *Tyrannosaurus rex,* but on closer examination the resemblance was slight. The creature had a tiny, wedge-shaped, almost feline head, a bull neck, and a wide, barrel-like chest. The three rows of spikes—which Will had at first thought were gigantic rocks—clattered as the creature towered over them.

Godzilla was almost completely motionless now—only his eyelids fluttered, and his lips curled back, to reveal six-foot-long bone-yellow teeth.

The monster stood on his hind legs, chest-deep in the churning waters of the Sea of Japan. Though Will could not judge the depth of the water here, he figured it must be close to two hundred feet deep.

That would make Godzilla over three hundred feet tall! he realized with amazed terror. Streams of seawater ran off of Godzilla's hide, giving the monster a slick shine.

Then Will heard a huge, sustained rush of air.

The creature must have just exhaled, he realized. Carefully, Will sniffed the air. An odor of fish and ozone permeated the atmosphere around the ferry. *I can smell it*, he said to himself.

Will was surprised to notice that Godzilla's body was not covered with scales—nor was it green. Instead, the creature was a dull charcoal black color, and his skin seemed gouged and pitted with deep vertical grooves. More than anything else, Godzilla's hide resembled the bark on an ancient oak tree. Will could swear that some of the grooves had barnacles, seaweed, and other sea life growing in the deepest furrows.

As Will watched, Godzilla slowly turned his mammoth body to the side. The huge spiked plates on his back slammed together, ringing like bronze church bells. This slow movement caused the water around Godzilla to churn even more.

Waves crashed against the damaged ferryboat with tremendous force. This action brought new screams of panic from the passengers, who still crowded the exits in a desperate attempt to flee from the monster.

Suddenly, there was another rush of air as Godzilla inhaled. Then a terrible, echoing roar smashed against Will's eardrums. As he covered his ears with his hands, Will's eyes rose until he was looking up at Godzilla's massive, feral head. To his shock and surprise, the great prehistoric monster seemed to be staring right back at him with a cold, reptilian gaze.

For a moment, the human and the monster locked eyes.

Then Will felt a tugging on his pant leg. He looked down. Soonji was clinging to his leg, her eyes wide, her tiny face pale with fear.

"Get down, Will," she whimpered, averting her eyes from the beast. "He *sees* you!"

The Maritime Self-Defense Force station near Hakata harbor in Japan was the first to receive the distress call from the Pusan ferry. Instantly, the duty officer sent out an emergency alert to the rescue choppers that were always on call.

Within minutes, three large, American-designed, single-rotor Sikorsky SH-60 "Seahawk" helicopters, built under license in Japan by Mitsubishi, were being powered up.

Also on the tarmac was a modified MH-53J "Sea Dragon" helicopter, bristling with antennas, with "Pave Low Enhanced" technology to enable it to lead a rescue or an attack in fog or in darkness. Like the rescue choppers, this highly advanced helicopter was always ready to launch at a moment's notice.

While the ground crews readied the aircraft, an officer burst from a nearby building, waving a clipboard in his hand. He ran to the MH-53J "Pave Low" helicopter's side door.

"Here are the exact coordinates of the ferry!" the officer cried over the sound of the spinning rotors. He handed the pilot the clipboard.

"Be advised—" the officer said, getting the pilot's attention by yanking on his flight suit.

"Yes!" the pilot barked impatiently, still studying his flight plan. "What is it?"

"The captain of the ship reports that he was attacked," the officer replied.

"Attacked!" the pilot said, both puzzled and excited. "Attacked by whom? The Communist Chinese? The North Koreans?"

"Worse than that," the officer replied.

Godzilla's roar echoed throughout the interior of the Pusan ferry, drowning out the screams of fear and panic.

"Come on...hurry!" Kim cried, tugging his mother's arm urgently. "We've got to get to the lifeboats!"

Kim's eyes, wide with dread, kept shifting from his fear-paralyzed mother to the panic-stricken crowds clogging the exits.

It was no use. Kim knew his mother was in the grip of her deepest fear—there was no way she would get on a lifeboat of her own free will.

It's up to me to save her, he decided.

On the other side of the passenger deck, Will Adams continued to peer out the window, straight into the eyes of the monster called Godzilla. And Soonji continued to tug on his leg.

Abruptly, Godzilla turned his mighty head, and the spell that seemed to paralyze the young American was broken. Will looked down at the young woman clinging to his leg.

"Come on, Soonji," he said, "let's get out of here."

Outside, Godzilla was slowly walking away from the disabled ferry. But the crew and passengers weren't out of danger yet. As the creature departed, Godzilla's tail swished back and forth, churning up the water. Some of the overcrowded rubber rafts that dotted the Sea of Japan were overturned in the turbulence. There were screams of terror as people fell into the sea and sank below the surface. Some would never rise again.

Another angry swish, and Godzilla sideswiped the ferry with his long, powerful tail. The whole ship vibrated like a drum. The tail struck again, and the side of the hull caved in. In the enclosed passenger deck, windows shattered, raining glass down on the people still trapped inside.

The Pusan ferry was looking less like a ship—and more like a soda can that had been crushed in the middle. And it was sinking fast.

Will struggled up from the deck and shook off pieces of broken glass. Everyone who was still aboard the ferry had been knocked off their feet when the ship was swatted by the monster's tail for the third time. Now the ferry was listing precariously to one side. Footing was difficult on the steeply pitched deck, but Will managed to remain standing.

He spotted Soonji, who was struggling to get up off the heaving deck. *This ship is going to capsize*, Will realized with horror.

He knew he had to get out and take Soonji with him. But people were still choking the exits. In their panic, the passengers were actually making escape through the doors all but impossible.

Then Will turned and saw the shattered windows. He grabbed Soonji by the hand and yanked her to her feet. She yelped in surprise as he dragged her toward the broken window. There was still some glass blocking their exit. Will pushed his shoulder hard against it, and the cracked window collapsed into shards. Most of the glass pitched into the sea, but some of it rained down on him. Blood began to flow from a cut on his forehead.

"Through here!" he cried, pushing the young woman.

Soonji was about to climb through the window when she saw a Korean boy tugging on an older woman's arm. The woman was curled up in a ball and utterly refused to let go of the heaving deck. Soonji pushed Will's hand away and pointed. He saw them, too.

Will rushed to Kim's side and grabbed the boy. As he lifted Kim over his shoulder, the boy started kicking and shouting. "Mother! What about my mother?" he cried.

Of course, Will didn't understand Korean, but he got the message. Before he could act, Soonji grabbed the woman's arm.

"Up, old mother," Soonji said in Korean.

"No!" the woman screamed. "I can't swim!"

But Soonji would hear none of it. She grabbed the woman by her hair and yanked upward. The woman hollered and jumped to her feet. Soonji dragged her to the window.

The ferry continued to sink. The ocean lapped against the hull only a few feet below the broken window. Will's eyes opened wide with hope when he saw an empty rubber raft bobbing in the water about thirty feet away. Will pulled the Korean boy off his shoulder and pointed to the raft.

"Can you swim?" he asked the boy. Will made swimming motions because the boy obviously didn't understand English. Kim got the message and nodded enthusiastically. At that moment, Soonji appeared at Will's side, dragging the Korean woman behind her.

"I can't swim!" the woman screamed again and again in shrill Korean. "I don't want to go into the water!"

Soonji and Will ignored her. While Kim watched open-mouthed, the couple lifted his mother up and placed her on the broken window sill—careful to avoid the spikes of glass that were still embedded in the frame. She resisted them with all of her strength.

Finally, Soonji had had enough! "Shut up, old mother," she cried. "Shut up...or I'll let you drown!"

When the woman heard the word *drown,* she began to scream and fight with new determination. Soonji turned and faced Will. He couldn't believe it when she actually smiled at him. "Watch this," she said in English.

Then Soonji put her foot on the struggling woman's rump and booted her over the side!

Before the screaming woman even hit the water, Soonji, Will, and Kim had dived over the side, too. In seconds, they were all splashing into the cold waters of the Sea of Japan.

Though Will thought of himself as a strong swimmer, it was hard trying to get to the inflatable raft. He squinted as salty sea water stung his eyes. The raft bobbed tantalizingly near, but the waves, which were violently churning in the wake of Godzilla's passage, kept pushing him back, toward the hull of the sinking ferry.

Exhausted, Will had to rest. He flipped over on

his back and tried floating in the rough waters. As he drifted, he could see Soonji, the Korean boy, and the boy's mother. They were huddled together in the water, clinging to a broken cable hanging over the side of the ferry.

Will noticed that the ship was sinking faster now. The sea had risen almost to the top of the hull. Soon the decks would be awash with water. If Will didn't get to the raft and rescue the others, they would be dragged to the bottom of the Sea of Japan by the suction of the huge sinking ferryboat.

With renewed determination, Will struck out again. He'd swum about halfway to the raft when another wave knocked him backward. Sputtering and swallowing water, Will reached out and grabbed blindly for something to keep him afloat. At last, his hands connected and he held on.

With a gasp, Will realized he was clutching the corpse of an old man—one of the passengers—who had already drowned. Will pulled back in horror and kicked the body away from him. He swam on frantically.

A few minutes later, gasping for breath, Will climbed aboard the empty raft. His arms and legs felt like lead, and he could barely lift himself to his elbows as he lay at the bottom of the bobbing rubber boat. Vaguely, he heard Soonji's voice in the distance. She was frantically screaming his name.

Will lifted himself up and saw the reason for her panic. The ferry was sinking very rapidly now. Waves were washing across its deck, and Soonji, Kim, and Kim's mother were barely able to hang on. The three of them were being battered by the sea.

Clambering up to a sitting position, Will searched the raft for oars. There were none, so he dropped to his belly on the side of the rubber raft and began using his tired arms as paddles. It seemed to take an eternity to move the raft close to the ferry, but Will managed it.

Weakly, he reached out for the others. Kim was the first aboard. The boy was able to swim the few feet to the raft and climb aboard. He helped Will and Soonji pull his mother onto the nearly swamped rubber boat. The woman was numb and paralyzed with fear—but thanks to Soonji and Kim, she was alive. Will cupped his hands and began bailing water out of the tiny, crowded raft.

Just then, an underwater explosion shook the ocean around them. The hull of the ferryboat shuddered. Smoke began pouring out of the windows and hatches as the ferry upended. The few passengers who had stubbornly remained aboard now jumped over the side, or were thrown overboard by the violent explosion.

As Kim, Soonji, and Will paddled away from the ship, using their arms as oars, the stern of the Pusan ferry lifted out of the water, and then the entire ship slipped beneath the waves.

As it disappeared, the ferry left a powerful whirlpool in its wake. Some of the people swimming were caught up in the swirling waters. Most of them were too weak from trying to stay afloat to even scream as they were sucked under.

For a terrifying instant, it felt as if the lifeboat was going to be sucked into the vortex, too. Kim's mother screamed as the raft was turned around by the whirlpool once, then twice. Finally, the swirling movement slowed and the raft—incredibly—remained floating on the surface.

After the noise and violence of the sinking, the silence that followed the disappearance of the ferryboat was eerie. Will, exhausted, peeked over the edge of the raft. In the distance, he could see Godzilla, still moving away from them. He watched for another minute, until the creature finally vanished into the haze and fog.

Then Will sank to the bottom of the raft, where he remained for the next half hour. He was tired, cold, sore, and dazed by his experience.

Will only looked up when, in the far distance, he heard the sound of rotors. *Helicopters!*

Will almost burst out laughing. He heard Soonji sob and whisper something in Korean to the little boy.

I can't believe it....We're saved! Will said to himself. But he only half-believed it.

Godzilla is still alive—and he's still out there.

CHAPTER 8

SPECIAL ASSIGNMENT

May 29, 1998, 2:29 P.M.
The newsroom, INN headquarters
Tokyo, Japan

Brian Shimura was happy that Nick's dire predictions about his life at INN had not been realized.

True, he had toiled in the mailroom, but only for two days. And he had worked as a fact checker for three more days. But, finally, at the end of his first week, Brian had been moved up to the newsroom and given some real journalistic duties.

At the moment, those duties consisted of sitting in his cubicle, watching a television screen that was tuned to a rival network—in this case, CNN. Brian's job was to monitor the broadcasts on the Cable News Network. If a story broke on CNN that was not covered by INN, Brian was supposed to notify Mr. Takao, the newsroom chief. Other interns, mostly Japanese, monitored NHK and some of the other Asian news networks.

Occasionally, a reporter would assign Brian to other jobs. Some of those jobs were interesting, others were a pain. But mostly Brian just watched television.

"You've got that glassy-eyed stare again," Nick said, tapping Brian on the shoulder. "Isn't it time for a break?"

Brian peeked at his watch and smiled. "That it is," he announced, pulling off his earphones.

"What's hot, newswise?" Nick asked as they headed to the break room together.

"Ohhh, well, the U.S. president is threatening trade sanctions against Japan again," Brian said. "The dollar is falling against the Japanese yen, the British pound, and the German mark; another baseball strike is looming, and Kevin Costner's new movie is getting panned by the critics."

"In other words, nothing," Nick replied.

"You said it," Brian agreed. "Sometimes I wonder why we bother becoming journalists. There's no *real* news to report. Nothing ever really happens."

"So you want to go out tonight?" Nick asked, changing the subject. "Yoshi's back. I'm sure he'd like to join us. How about midnight karaoke?"

Brian groaned as he yawned. "You know, Nick," he said earnestly, "you got to sleep in this morning—the *third* morning in a row."

"My job stinks," Nick replied defensively. "Lacks Pulse is a real pain to work for—and *he* doesn't get in until noon!"

"Mr. *Hulse* is management," Brian explained. "*You* are not."

"That'll change when my talent is finally recognized," Nick stated. "Now what about midnight karaoke?"

"No way," Brian insisted.

"Come on!" Nick urged him. "It'll be fun. You haven't lived until you've seen a middle-aged

Japanese businessman singing 'Gypsies, Tramps, and Thieves' just like Cher."

"Don't be so sure," Brian replied. "I've already seen my parents dance the hokey-pokey at my sister's wedding."

"The horror…the horror," Nick replied, pretending to shudder.

"Shimura-san! Gordon-san!" a voice cried from behind them. Both youths turned. One of the Japanese interns was running down the hall, calling them.

"Come quick! To the newsroom. Big news!" he cried.

Brian and Nick took off in a run back toward the INN newsroom. The whole place was jammed with people—and it had been practically empty only a few moments ago. Now all eyes were on the overhead television screens, which usually monitored the INN network satellite feeds from dozens of remote locations.

All the screens showed the same image—Japanese military helicopters circling over a section of ocean, plucking people out of the water.

Brian tapped Yoshi. "What's going on?" he asked.

"The Pusan ferry, which runs from Japan to Korea, has sunk," he said, his eyes never leaving the television screens.

"So these are *live* shots?" Nick asked.

"*Hai*," Yoshi replied, nodding his head. Nick turned to peek at the television monitors at the desks—the ones tuned to the other news networks. On CNN there was a commercial for deodorant. NHK had a Japanese game show.

"Pretty dramatic stuff," Nick said. "And it looks

like we've got an exclusive." He pointed to the other monitors.

Yoshi shook his head. "This is not going out over the satellite feeds," he replied. "The live footage we are seeing is being recorded, but it is not being broadcast on the air."

Nick and Brian were shocked. "Why not?" Nick cried. His journalistic sensibilities were outraged.

"Because the Japanese government doesn't *want* it to be broadcast, that's why!" a voice announced behind them.

Nick, Yoshi, and Brian turned. Other reporters and INN staffers turned, too. Some even began to protest with indignant voices.

Everett P. Endicott raised his pudgy arms and silenced them all. May McGovern was at his side, looking grim. "An official news blackout is in effect," Endicott said in a voice loud enough to be heard over the commotion.

"No live footage of this disaster is to be broadcast at the present time. This is a request from the Japanese government that INN officials have decided to grant."

People began shouting questions, drowning each other out.

"We're not going to be scooped," Endicott reassured them. "The other networks got the message, too."

"What's *really* going on, Everett?" Blackthorn Adams shouted from his office doorway.

"I don't know yet," Endicott replied. "Everything is on a need-to-know basis—and right now, we don't need to know!"

There were more moans and groans. Endicott's voice cut through the newsroom protests. "The Japanese government has promised to hold a press conference later this afternoon at the Diet Building, outside of the parliament's chambers. INN will be sending some of you to cover that event.

"That is all we know for now."

With that, Endicott turned his wide behind on the room and ponderously waddled toward the elevators. He left a shocked and mostly speechless newsroom staff behind him.

"It must be something really big to get that tub of lard out of his office and down here with the peons," Nick said to Brian.

"That's enough out of you, Nick Gordon!" May spat angrily. Yoshi suddenly walked away, embarrassed by May's emotional outburst. Brian didn't know what to make of her hostile reaction whenever Nick was around. She seemed nice enough to everyone else.

To Brian's surprise, Nick said nothing to her in reply. He just headed toward his cubicle in silence.

When Nick was gone, May approached Brian and waved Yoshi over to her side, too. "This is for you," she said, handing Brian an envelope. He looked at her and she put her finger to her lips. "Keep your mouth shut," she whispered. Then she handed an identical envelope to Yoshi.

"I'll see you both later," she said over her shoulder as she departed.

Brian and Yoshi watched May head for the elevators. Then Brian turned to the Japanese youth. "What was *that* all about?" he asked.

"These?" Yoshi asked, holding up his envelope.

"No," Brian replied. "I mean her reaction to Nick!"

Yoshi looked puzzled for a second. Then he nodded his head in understanding. "Ah, you mean the way Ms. McGovern speaks to Nick—always angry, always rude?" he replied.

"Yeah," Brian nodded.

"You did not know that they used to—what is the word?—step out together?" Yoshi replied.

"You mean they used to *date?*" Brian asked, stunned. Nick had never mentioned it.

"Hai." Yoshi nodded rapidly. "They used to date. Big romance!"

Brian smiled and shook his head. "I should have known," he said aloud. "May is about the only woman at INN that Nick *doesn't* talk about."

"Just so." Yoshi nodded. "Deep feelings between them have caused much unseemly anger and hostility."

"What happened?" Brian asked. "Why did they stop seeing each other?"

"Nick broke it off. He said she became a big sellout," Yoshi replied. "She went to work for Boss Gaijin. Nick didn't like that too much."

Brian nodded again. "That sounds like Nick," he said. Then Brian remembered the envelope in his hand. "Excuse me," he said to Yoshi. "I have to read my mail."

"So must I," Yoshi said.

Brian rushed back to his cubicle. When no one else was looking, he examined the envelope. On the outside, next to his name, were bold red letters: CONFIDENTIAL—FOR YOUR EYES ONLY. Brian ripped it open. There was a single page inside, with a terse message.

> *Mr. Shimura:*
> *Please report to my office at six o'clock. I have a special assignment for you.*
> *Everett P. Endicott.*

Brian's heart raced. *A special assignment—at last!*

At precisely six o'clock, Brian stepped into Everett P. Endicott's outer office. May McGovern was sitting behind her desk, speaking urgently into the phone. She nodded to Brian when he entered, and motioned for him to sit down. Brian was not surprised to see Yoshi sitting in the opposite chair.

As May continued her phone conversation in a hushed tone, Brian leaned over to Yoshi. "Do you know what's going on?" he asked. Yoshi shook his head nervously.

At that moment, May hung up the phone. Without a word to Brian or Yoshi, she leaped to her feet and rushed into Endicott's inner office and closed the door behind her. Brian leaned back in his chair and tried to relax.

The minutes ticked by. Brian looked at his watch.

Then the door swung open and May ushered Brian and Yoshi into Endicott's inner sanctum. The office was just as Brian remembered it. The only difference was that the blinds were closed, blocking out the dramatic view of Tokyo at twilight.

The big man was sitting behind his desk. His baby face was creased with worry when he looked up at them.

"Sorry for the secrecy," Endicott said. "Sit down, boys."

Brian and Yoshi took seats.

"In a little while, two men will be arriving here. They are a small part of the biggest story of this, or any, century," Endicott announced dramatically.

Brian and Yoshi looked at each other.

"Originally, I was going to have you both assist Blackthorn Adams in working with these men." Endicott paused. "Unfortunately, Ms. McGovern informs me that Blackthorn's son was one of the survivors pulled out of the Sea of Japan after that ferry wreck early this morning...so Blackthorn won't be joining us.

"He's on his way to Hakata and has asked for some time off, which means that we'll have to make do with the resources we have." Endicott looked up at May.

"Call Nick Gordon and tell him to come up here immediately," Endicott told her.

"*Mister* Endicott!" May exclaimed. "You can't trust *him* with a story like this. It's too—too *big!* Call the network. Surely they can send *someone!*"

"I agree with your assessment of Mr. Gordon," Endicott said. "However, in another hour or two, the whole world is going to be in an uproar..."

For the second time, Brian and Yoshi traded glances. *This is something very, very big,* Brian thought, suddenly queasy.

"Every reporter in the world will be working on

his or her own angle," Endicott continued. "We have a chance at an exclusive here, and we have a responsibility to our network and our viewers. INN needs a science correspondent on this story, so call Mr. Gordon, please."

May did not argue further. She tossed her long auburn hair and headed for her desk. But when she left her boss's office, she closed the door behind her a little too hard. Endicott sighed again.

"Excuse me for a moment," he said to Brian and Yoshi. Then he lifted the cover off of his laptop computer and began to type. Five silent and uncomfortable minutes later, there was a knock at the door.

"Come in," Endicott said, closing his computer.

"Hiya, chief," Nick said, stepping into the room wearing a cocky smile. "You called?"

"Sit down, Gordon," Endicott said, pointing to an empty chair. Nick sat down, flashing a toothy grin at Brian and Yoshi. May stepped into the office and closed the door behind her. Endicott looked at the four of them, and then spoke.

"The Pusan ferry sank this morning," he began. "Casualties were moderate, mostly because the captain got out an early distress call. But the real scoop here is that the ferry was *attacked*."

Endicott paused dramatically to gauge their surprised reactions. "The ferry was attacked by the prehistoric monster called Godzilla."

Nick's grin disappeared. Brian looked at Yoshi, who paled visibly. May nodded, her face serious. Finally, Brian cleared his throat and spoke.

"But Godzilla is supposed to be dead," he said.

"Well, it seems reports of Godzilla's death have been greatly exaggerated," Endicott replied. At that moment, his telephone buzzed. Endicott lifted the receiver. "Yes!" he barked.

Endicott listened for a moment then nodded. "Send them up," he said and hung up.

"They're here, May," Endicott said to his assistant. May rose and left the room.

"The Japanese government is about to announce Godzilla's return," Endicott continued. "The network brass has ordered me to assign a science correspondent and a cameraman to cover the activities of the two men you are about to meet."

"Why?" Nick asked seriously. "Who *are* these guys?"

"'These guys' are among the world's only experts on Godzilla—if there can be such a thing," Endicott replied. "These two men, and dozens of others, have worked together in total secrecy for over forty years, preparing for the possible return of the monster."

"If their work was so secret," Brian interrupted, "how come we know about them?"

"A fair question," Endicott said. "A few years ago, one of these men retired from his government's service. His name is Dr. Hiroshi Nobeyama—"

"The molecular biologist who won the Nobel in 1997?" Nick interrupted.

"The very same," Endicott nodded. "Dr. Nobeyama has been working as a scientific consultant for our parent company, International Science Systems. But this afternoon, when it was learned that Godzilla had returned, he was recalled to active duty to head a special defense task force established by the Japanese government during this crisis.

"Dr. Nobeyama has, of course, agreed to help but requested that INN be given exclusive coverage of his group's activities. To everyone's amazement, the government has agreed to this."

Endicott paused, scanning the three youthful faces before him. "It is a remarkable opportunity, gentlemen," he said. "You will be at the very center of the crisis, for as long as it lasts."

"Why *us?*" Nick asked, clearly excited by the prospect. "Why not Max Hulse?"

"Max Hulse stays in Tokyo. He is doing our on-camera work," Endicott replied. "And if it were up to me, *you* would not be here, Mr. Gordon. *You* are merely a replacement for Blackthorn Adams—and not a very good one, in my estimation."

"Yeah, I like you, too," Nick shot back. Endicott ignored the insubordination.

"Mr. Masahara is here because he is one of our best new field cameramen—*and* I can almost spare him."

Endicott's eyes fell on Brian. "Mr. Shimura is a special case. *He* is here because his services were specifically requested."

"The network wants *me?*" Brian asked.

Just then, the door swung open behind Brian. Yoshi and Nick jumped to their feet. Everett P. Endicott rose, too. Brian saw that May McGovern was ushering two men into the room. Leading the way was a distinguished-looking Japanese man with gray hair and horn-rimmed glasses. Brian could not see the second man, who was still behind the door, but he heard him speak.

"It's not the network that wants you, son," a familiar voice announced with a slight Texas drawl. "*I* want you."

Brian's eyes widened in amazement as a giant of an American with an erect, military bearing stepped into the room.

"Uncle Maxwell!" Brian cried out in astonishment.

CHAPTER 9

ALL IN THE FAMILY

May 29, 1998, 6:55 P.M.
Office of the Japanese bureau chief
Independent News Network
Tokyo, Japan

Standing next to Brian, Nick couldn't resist the urge. He reached out, put his hand under his roommate's chin, and pushed Brian's mouth closed. Brian blinked, then shook himself out of his astonishment.

Meanwhile, a tall, imposing figure entered the room. He wore a tailored U.S. Navy dress blue uniform. His dark hair was streaked with silver, and his face had been lined by sun, salt-spray, and harsh weather. Despite his stern, craggy features, the man Brian called "Uncle Maxwell" had an engaging smile. He extended his hand to Everett P. Endicott, who came around his desk to meet him.

"Admiral Maxwell B. Willis, United States Navy," he said, gripping the portly man's hand.

"Pleased to meet you, Admiral," Endicott said smoothly. "*Now* I understand why Brian's services were specifically requested," the bureau chief said. Admiral Willis winked. "My nephew's been in Japan almost three weeks, and he didn't even call. I figured he was avoiding me, and so I thought I'd get his attention."

There was a ripple of laughter that broke the tension in the now-crowded office. The admiral reached out and touched the older Japanese man on the shoulder.

"May I introduce my friend and colleague, Dr. Hiroshi Nobeyama."

The Japanese man bowed graciously, and after introductions were completed, the men—and May—got down to business.

"Two days from now, on May 31, a joint task force of Japanese Navy ships and elements of the United States Air Force stationed in Korea are going to launch a preemptive strike against Godzilla."

May gasped. Nick whooped in surprise.

"This must be done while Godzilla is still in the relatively shallow waters of the Sea of Japan," Admiral Willis told his amazed listeners.

"Of course," he added, "this information is top secret, and must not leave this room—for now. *Officially,* there will be an emergency meeting of the United Nations tomorrow, where all this will be hashed out by the Security Council in the public eye. *Unofficially,* I can tell you that this attack is a done deal. It *will* take place. Period."

"How do you know where Godzilla is?" May McGovern asked. Nick noted that her long-dormant reporter's instinct was returning.

"Helicopters equipped with sonar systems, as

well as two *Yuushio*-class submarines of the Japanese Maritime Self-Defense Force, have been stalking Godzilla since his appearance this morning," the admiral answered.

"What's the hurry?" Endicott blurted. "Maybe Godzilla won't even come ashore. Why ask for trouble?"

It was Dr. Nobeyama who answered. "It does not matter whether or not Godzilla comes ashore," he said. "The monster will do great damage no matter where he goes. We *know* Godzilla wrecked the Pusan ferry. Several other ships have also been reported missing."

"Why now?" Nick asked, his curiosity aroused. "What made Wonder Lizard return to life, or wake up from hibernation, or whatever he did?"

Dr. Nobeyama smiled at the youth. "Two years ago, a Russian submarine was lost off the coast of China. Several weeks before that, the French government conducted the first open nuclear tests in the Pacific Ocean in many years—"

"We think that Godzilla was awakened by those French hydrogen bomb tests in 1996," Admiral Willis interrupted.

"Yes," Dr. Nobeyama nodded. "At first the creature was probably weak—Godzilla feeds on nuclear radiation, you see. The French nuclear tests were powerful enough to awaken him, but not powerful enough to return Godzilla to his full strength. That is why he attacked the Russian nuclear submarine—"

"Sea Base One!" It was Nick who interrupted this time. "Sea Base One discovered the wreckage of that sub. They *knew* Godzilla had sunk it!"

"You're sharp, son,"Admiral Willis said. "Sea Base One found the nuclear core from that sunken submarine. And it was drained of all nuclear energy. Hell! It wasn't even radioactive anymore."

"You mean that Godzilla is capable of absorbing nuclear energy?" Nick asked. "That he actually feeds on it?"

"Probably not exclusively," Dr. Nobeyama answered. "Godzilla has a stomach and a heart, lungs, blood, probably a liver. Godzilla is physically capable of eating more traditional fare.

"But to survive long-term, and to be able to use his most destructive offensive weapon—his so-called radioactive breath—Godzilla must replenish his supply of radioactive material from time to time."

"You see,"Admiral Willis spoke again, "Godzilla is a radioactive creature. He's not really a dinosaur, although he probably *was* a dinosaur once. But now, after the exposure to radiation that created him, Godzilla is more like a living, breathing nuclear fusion reactor."

Dr. Nobeyama nodded in agreement. "Godzilla is a creature capable of generating tremendous power, but like a reactor, he needs raw nuclear material to start the process—"

"So you're saying that once Godzilla absorbs enough radiation, he becomes self-sufficient," May said, finishing the doctor's thought.

The Japanese scientist nodded and smiled sagely. "You are correct, young lady," he said. "Godzilla is alive now, and active. But we believe that the creature still lacks enough radioactive material to achieve full strength."

Admiral Willis leaned forward in his chair. "We—Dr. Nobeyama and I—are certain that Godzilla will come ashore in Japan. We think Godzilla is looking for radioactive material to consume, the way he consumed that Russian sub's nuclear core—"

"And Japan has more nuclear reactors than any other country in the world!" Nick broke in, slapping himself on the forehead.

"Indeed!" Yoshi nodded. "The monster wants to feed on one of our nuclear reactors—or perhaps more than one."

"And we must stop him before he does!" Admiral Willis declared. "Right now. Before he reaches land."

"But will conventional weapons be effective against Godzilla?" Brian asked. "If I remember correctly, they didn't work the last time."

Dr. Nobeyama and Admiral Willis were silent for a moment. Then Dr. Nobeyama spoke. "In my opinion, the weapons that the Navy is planning to use—bombs, missiles, cannon shells, machine-gun bullets—will *not* work," he said with emotion.

Admiral Willis nodded his head in agreement. "But until the governments of the world actually *see* conventional weapons fail, they will not believe their weapons are useless," he said.

"Why are you so sure modern weapons *will* fail?" Nick argued. "Do you have scientific proof?"

Again, Nobeyama and the American exchanged glances. "I would rather not make my theories known until I have more...evidence," the old

Japanese man said cryptically.

"But you've tried to convince them that weapons won't work, haven't you?" Endicott asked.

"Of course," Admiral Willis drawled, shaking his head. "But the boys in the Puzzle Palace—er, the *Pentagon*—have a thousand different excuses. They say our bombs are better now, our weapons are more powerful, they're smarter, and on and on."

"My government, too, has become overconfident," Dr. Nobeyama said. "They do not remember the last time Godzilla came, or they choose to forget."

"What about nukes?" Nick suggested. "A hydrogen bomb dropped on his head might give Godzilla more than a migraine! It would probably vaporize him."

Dr. Nobeyama and Admiral Willis exchanged glances once again, but neither of them spoke.

The little INN meeting continued into the evening. At nine o'clock, Admiral Willis rose. "I think that about wraps things up for now," he announced, stifling a yawn.

"Tomorrow morning my assistant will arrive and supply you with some additional material on Godzilla," Dr. Nobeyama added. "I hope you can spare her some facilities—a videotape machine, an overhead projector, tape recorders."

"That can easily be arranged, Doctor," Endicott said. "Ms. McGovern will set up a conference room for your assistant's exclusive use."

"That's fine, Mr. Endicott." Admiral Willis added, "I think it's important for these young people to be brought up to speed." The Admiral turned to Nick, Brian, and Yoshi. "Pack your bags, boys. Tomorrow you'll take a helicopter to the Sea of Japan and link up with the Japanese forces. We'll bunk you on our research vessel tomorrow night. That'll give you twenty-four hours to get your sea legs."

As the meeting broke up, Admiral Willis approached Brian and slapped his nephew on the back. "Excited, boy?" he said with a smile.

"Something like that," Brian said nervously. He couldn't believe what was happening. This morning he'd woken up an unimportant intern at a small news network, and now he was in the middle of the biggest news story since World War II!

"It's the chance of a lifetime," the older man said.

Brian smiled. "And I thank you for it, Uncle Maxwell," he replied gratefully.

"Don't mention it, Brian," the admiral said. "I...I wanted to make it up to you. I'm just sorry about what happened...and I'm sorry I couldn't make it back for your mother's funeral. She was a great lady..."

Brian felt a rush of affection for his gruff *gaijin* uncle. "Thanks," he simply replied.

On the other side of the office, Nick cornered May.

"You almost sounded like a *real* journalist for a minute there," he said. "Not some *secretary* who arranges conference rooms and makes coffee for the big boys."

May glared at Nick but did not reply to his barbed comments.

"Oh, I understand," Nick continued boldly. "If

you suck up enough, someday you'll get a corner office with the parent company. You might even make CEO—but it's a waste!"

"Why?" May snapped back. "What's wrong with having a little ambition? I've told you over and over again, I don't *want* to get down in the mud and grope for stories anymore."

"And *I* remember that quote by Shakespeare," Nick said with a smile. "Something about a woman protesting too much—"

"Don't forget your air-sickness pills," May said with a nasty sneer on her pretty face. "Remember the *last* time you were in a helicopter."

Nick quaked, nearly turning green from the mere memory as May quickly left the office.

The next morning, Brian was awakened by a knock at the door. When he answered it, one of the Japanese interns handed him a box. Brian thanked the man, then closed the door and opened the package.

Inside, he found a note from Uncle Maxwell.

Brian,
Here are a couple of things to look at before
Lieutenant Takado arrives for your briefing.

Brian found a hardcover book, three videocassettes, and an ancient issue of *Life* magazine inside a clear plastic envelope. The magazine, dated 1955, featured a black-and-white photo of Godzilla on the cover. It was an eerie image of the creature's head photographed through a gigantic cage filled with wildly panicked birds. Brian actually shivered when he looked at the strange, powerful photograph.

The book, of course, was famous. Brian already had a copy in his bedroom back in Los Angeles: *This Is Tokyo* was written by Chicago journalist Stephen Martin, an eyewitness to Godzilla's 1954 attack on Japan's capital city.

Like John Hersey's *Hiroshima* and Bob Woodward and Carl Bernstein's *All the President's Men,* Martin's book was a standard volume for journalism students to study. Brian had read it when he was twelve years old. He still remembered parts of *This Is Tokyo* vividly.

The three videotapes were identified by labels. One tape was of the Godzilla episode of the PBS show *Nova.* Brian remembered seeing it when he was a teenager. The show featured documentary footage of Godzilla and interviews with the survivors of the monster's first attack.

The second tape was a commercial videocassette of the 1956 docudrama adapted from Stephen Martin's book. The movie, sensationally retitled *Godzilla, King of the Monsters,* featured studio footage of actors mixed with real documentary footage of the actual destruction of Tokyo. Brian recalled seeing this film as well. Raymond Burr portrayed Stephen Martin. That same actor had later played Perry Mason and Ironside on television.

The third tape was more personal. It was a copy of some of Uncle Maxwell's home movies, including Brian's and his sister's high school graduations and shots from his sister's wedding. Brian put this tape aside for now.

"What's in the box, Brian?" Nick asked, yawning.

"Just some stuff Uncle Maxwell sent over," Brian replied. "Stuff about Godzilla."

Nick picked up the book. "Oh, man," he said. "I read this Martin guy during my freshman year in journalism...*This Is Tokyo,* or how not to write a book. What a hack!"

"Yeah, well, he won a Pulitzer Prize, you know," Brian observed.

Nick nodded. "Sure he did. But those were the good old days of broadcast journalism. All you had to say was, 'Oh, the humanity' or 'That's the way it is' or some other vapid cliché, and you were enshrined as an immortal god of journalism. That was then. *This* is now," Nick argued. "Stephen Martin is just too weepy and sentimental for modern tastes."

Leafing through the pages, Nick shook his head.

"My God, just listen to this guy's prose..." He began to read from the book in a pretentious voice.

"'This is Tokyo,'" Nick intoned, "'a smoldering memorial to the unknown. An unknown that at this very moment still prevails, and could, at any time, lash out with its terrible destruction anywhere else in the world. There were once many people here who could have told what they saw. Now there are only a few...'"

Nick held his nose theatrically. "Stink-a-rino!" he snorted. He flipped through more pages.

"How about *this* one?" Nick continued. "'I'm saying a prayer, George. A prayer for the whole world.'" He slammed the book shut in exasperation.

"Yeeesshhh, what crap!" he concluded.

"You're right. Times *were* different then," Brian replied. "Journalists had much different standards. They weren't supposed to be totally objective—they reported the news, but they were *allowed* to show a little bit of emotion."

"Whatever," Nick replied. He glanced at the digital clock on the front of the VCR.

"We're supposed to get briefed at ten-thirty," he said. "I'm gonna take a shower." Nick dropped the book, turned, and headed for the bathroom.

When his roommate was gone, Brian picked up the book and began reading.

CHAPTER 10

NIGHT FLIGHT

May 30, 1998, 7:55 P.M.
Aboard a U.S. Navy MH-53E "Sea Dragon"
   helicopter
Somewhere over the Sea of Japan

The ride was bumpy, the noise was horrendous,
but the smell was the worst.

Nick had been heaving into a sickness bag for
the past hour. Unfortunately, in the jittering chopper, which was buffeted about by winds coming
off the ocean, he was missing the bag more than he
was hitting it. The mess was beginning to nauseate
everyone else riding the helicopter.

Brian lifted his eyes from the book he was reading and exchanged an amused glance with Yoshi.
The Japanese cameraman sat opposite Brian in the
metal hammocks that passed for chairs in the military helicopter. His cameras, packed in steel cases,
were strapped in next to him.

Sitting beside Brian, across from Yoshi, was Dr.
Nobeyama's assistant, Lieutenant Emiko Takado.
She wore the dress uniform of the Japanese Self-
Defense Force, and the three men couldn't help

but notice that she wore the uniform *very* well. They wondered if her skirt was a little shorter than regulation length.

They had met Emiko—Lieutenant Takado—that morning, when she arrived at INN headquarters. She'd been sent by Dr. Nobeyama to brief them on theories concerning the origin and physiology of Godzilla.

Yoshi, especially, had been surprised to see that Dr. Nobeyama's assistant was a member of Japan's Self-Defense Force—and a woman at that. The Japanese military was not as open to female recruits as the armies of many other countries. *She must be a very remarkable woman,* he thought with admiration.

Yoshi suddenly realized that the lieutenant had caught him staring at her. He turned his head away shyly.

Emiko's expression remained fixed, but she smiled to herself behind the mirrored sunglasses.

The noise, and the shaking of the chopper, made it next to impossible for Brian to read Stephen Martin's account of the destruction of Tokyo. The copy of *This Is Tokyo* his uncle had sent him was a recent edition, reprinted after Martin's death in 1994. Unfortunately, Brian hadn't even finished reading the in-depth introduction by Carl Sagan.

He sighed, stretched, and shut the book. He tucked it into a travel bag and settled back into the metal-and-canvas chair. As the military helicopter raced over the Sea of Japan, Brian closed his eyes and let his mind drift back to the briefing that morning.

*   *   *

"Godzilla first appeared off the shore of Oto Island in August 1954," Lieutenant Takado had said that morning, as a grainy black-and-white photo flashed onto the white projection screen. It was a picture of Godzilla, his head and much of his torso peeking over a hill. In the foreground of the photograph, Brian noticed several humans, fleeing in panic.

It's a cliché, he thought, *but they look like ants.*

Brian looked away from the screen and scanned the other faces in the room.

Nick Gordon, Yoshi Masahara, and May McGovern sat around a huge table in the INN conference room. Their eyes were glued to the screen at the front of the room. Each member of the INN team had a folder open in front of them. It was filled with dozens of pages of text, mathematical formulas, graphs, and diagrams.

"The creature's origin is still a mystery," Lieutenant Takado continued. "But the nuclear physicists Dr. Edward Teller and Albert Einstein formulated the most likely theory…"

She clicked a remote control she held, and the image on the screen changed. An even grainier, and very blurry, photograph of a large reptile walking near a line of palm trees flashed onto the screen.

"In the 1940s, during the closing days of World War II, a mysterious species of reptile was reported by Japanese troops stationed in the Marshall Islands, a chain of small islands and atolls southwest of Hawaii.

"This photograph was taken in 1944 by a platoon of Japanese soldiers—none of whom survived the war, unfortunately. For years this photo was discounted as a hoax, or as wartime propaganda—until the appearance of Godzilla in 1954.

"Dr. Teller postulated that this animal, or another member of the species, was exposed to massive amounts of radiation from the first hydrogen bomb test on Bikini Atoll. The creature absorbed the radiation, and that caused it to mutate into the monster the western press calls Godzilla—"

"Excuse me…what do you mean by 'the western press'?" Nick interrupted.

Lieutenant Takado turned to Nick. "The Oto Islanders have a legend about a sea monster called Gojira. The word *Gojira,* translated into English, literally means 'whale ape'—or, more precisely, 'whale that walks upright like an ape.'

"When the mutation arrived on their shores in 1954, the islanders naturally mistook the radioactive monster for their mythical Gojira.

"It was the American journalist Stephen Martin who mistranslated the name into English as Godzilla. That name was adopted worldwide, though in Japan we still call the monster Gojira. There is, of course, a Latin name—"

"Spare us!" Nick cried with a dismissive wave. Brian snickered. He recalled that Nick wasn't very proficient in Latin.

Lieutenant Takado smiled, and clicked the control in her left hand. A full body shot of Godzilla flashed onto the screen. It, too, was in black and white.

"Godzilla is roughly 100 meters tall," she continued. "That's about 330 feet, or the size of a thirty-story building. His weight is estimated at about 65,000 metric tons. That makes Godzilla the largest living creature to ever walk or swim on this planet.

"Despite his incredible size, Godzilla can swim in excess of forty knots. He can move across land at nearly fifty kilometers an hour—though he usually moves at a considerably slower pace."

She clicked the control again. This time the image of Godzilla was in color. Nick realized it was a photograph taken only hours after Godzilla had wrecked the Pusan ferry.

"Godzilla's most formidable weapon is not his speed or size, however, but his ability to project a radioactive blast from his mouth. This blast is devastating. It can melt steel and concrete. Flesh is literally vaporized. The people aboard the ferry were very fortunate that the creature did not utilize this weapon."

"Why *didn't* Godzilla blast the ferry?" Brian asked.

Lieutenant Takado nodded. "A good question," she replied. "Dr. Nobeyama thinks that Godzilla had been asleep, floating in the Sea of Japan, perhaps for days. The ferry collided with him and woke him up.

"As to why he didn't attack the ferry...perhaps the creature did not identify the ship as a significant threat."

"Maybe it was just dumb luck," Nick muttered.

"Indeed," Lieutenant Takado said, nodding in agreement.

"Okay," Brian said, leaning forward. "So he's a big, fire-breathing dinosaur. How dangerous *is* he, really?"

"Several ships have been reported missing in the last three weeks," she replied. "And, of course, Godzilla sank the Russian submarine two years ago. As a maritime threat alone, Godzilla is more destructive than a typhoon."

Lieutenant Takado paused again, giving them more time to absorb the information. Then she clicked the control in her hand. A new image appeared. This one showed Godzilla crashing through the Diet—the Japanese parliamentary building—in 1954.

"Godzilla last entered a populated area—Tokyo, Japan—on November 3, 1954. On that night and the next, 179,000 people were killed. Another 30,000 were injured. Some people sustained radiation burns on much of their bodies. Godzilla's initial attack was followed by an outbreak of radiation sickness.

"The creature destroyed the Japanese seat of government and much of the capital city. He leveled buildings and crushed whole industries. Landmarks and shrines that were hundreds of years old were destroyed in a single night. The damage was in the hundreds of billions of yen. It took nearly a decade to rebuild the city…and so much more was lost for all time."

Lieutenant Takado began clicking the remote rapidly. A succession of images flashed across the screen, and then disappeared: black-and-white photographs of buildings in ruins, whole city blocks burning, hundreds of injured people choking hospital hallways and parks and sidewalks.

And then there were the pictures of the dead. Thousands of them. Bodies lining streets. Lying under shrouds. And sprawling where they fell. Burned. Crushed. Torn asunder.

Brian gulped and averted his eyes. Nick whistled softly. Yoshi turned pale. May looked sick.

"Godzilla is more destructive than the hydrogen bomb that gave him life," Lieutenant Takado said. "If the creature comes to land, there is no telling how much damage he will cause. Or how many people he will kill and injure."

"We'll be landing in five minutes," one of the helicopter crewmen shouted over the noise of the engine. Nick, who had his head buried between his knees, looked up. A relieved expression appeared on his pallid face. Yoshi nodded, his thoughts unreadable, as usual.

Brian turned and peered out of the tiny window. All he could see was dark water far below. But, as the crewman predicted, the Sea Dragon's wheels touched the brightly lit deck of a small ship five minutes later. As the rotors wound down, the door on the side of the helicopter slid open. Admiral Maxwell Willis stood on the deck to greet them.

"Permission to come aboard, sir," Lieutenant Takado said, saluting smartly.

"Permission granted," the admiral replied, returning her salute. Then he stood aside. "Welcome to the *Kongo-Maru*," he cried over the sound of the chopper's engine.

The Kongo-Maru, Brian thought, recalling the briefing that morning. According to Lieutenant Takado, the ship was a hastily built miracle, a specially constructed and fully outfitted research vessel designed to study and record any and all data on the creature called Godzilla.

The name itself was significant. *Maru,* of course, simply meant "ship;" the word was attached to almost all Japanese seagoing vessels. The word *kongo* had more meaning. The *kongo* was a legendary trident-shaped staff of knowledge from Japanese mythology. The *kongo* brought mankind wisdom and insight and pierced the darkness of ignorance.

And so this ship was created to shed light on the mystery that is Godzilla. Brian recalled Lieutenant Takado's earlier comment. She'd explained that the *Kongo-Maru* started life as a *Pegasus*-class combat patrol hydrofoil in the service of the U.S. Navy. The vessel was chosen because of its incredible speed—almost fifty knots when foilborne—and its amazing maneuverability.

The 145-foot hull was gutted from stem to stern for the purposes of its new mission. All weapons systems and defensive armaments were removed and replaced with dozens of monitoring devices.

Radiation detectors, microwave transmitters and receivers, radar, sonar—even sophisticated MRI imaging systems—were all retrofitted into the hydrofoil hull. Then a whole new superstructure was built over it. The size of the bridge was tripled to fit all the sophisticated instrumentation.

Much of the work had been done in the last two weeks. When Brian stepped off the chopper, he could see men still busily working in the rigging towers, on satellite dishes, and near the many antennas that stuck out of the ship's superstructure like porcupine needles.

As Brian, Nick, Yoshi, and Lieutenant Takado followed Admiral Willis onto the superstructure, the Sea Dragon—freed of its passengers—lifted into the air and flew off into the night. Crewmen immediately began folding up the collapsible helipad.

Brian was stunned by how cramped the *Kongo-Maru* really was. When the group stepped onto an extremely narrow walkway, he searched the bow of the ship. He wanted to get a glimpse of the boldest device on the *Kongo-Maru,* and potentially the most dangerous piece of equipment to use.

Brian wanted to see the harpoon.

"The bow of the ship is fitted with a hydraulic harpoon gun," Lieutenant Takado had told them earlier that day. "The harpoon itself is really an array of monitoring devices. If we can get close enough, the harpoon will be fired into Godzilla's flesh. For as long as the harpoon is connected to the ship by its fiber-optic cable, we will be able to take readings of Godzilla's vital signs.

"If the attack fails, then we *must* use the harpoon, or all our efforts will be wasted."

"What's the effective range of the harpoon gun?" Nick had asked. Brian recalled that Lieutenant Takado ignored that question. And he nervously concluded they'd have to get really close to use it.

Admiral Willis led the group through a steel door into the ship's interior. Then he excused himself.

"I've got to help calibrate some of the instruments," the admiral told them. "Lieutenant Takado'll show y'all to your quarters." The admiral also suggested they visit the lounge at their first opportunity.

"We have satellite feeds coming in from all over the world," he told them. "Since y'all are newshounds, you might want to watch some television and gauge the rest of the world's reaction to the return of Godzilla."

Brian already knew some of that reaction.

The prime minister of Japan had yesterday issued a statement to the world. It read, in part: "Godzilla has already taken human lives. This creature is a danger, not only to Japan, but to every nation in the world. I call upon the United Nations to do their part to help in this international emergency…"

The United Nations did their part, all right, Brian thought bitterly. *They argued, and they're still arguing.*

Lieutenant Takado led them down a ladder to the bowels of the ship. They walked through narrow corridors until they came to a hallway lined with doors. She opened a small door to reveal a tiny room with three bunks, one on top of the other. The room was hardly bigger than Brian's closet back at INN headquarters.

"I got dibs on the top bunk!" Nick announced, grinning.

Twenty minutes later, Brian led Nick and Yoshi back to where he thought the lounge was. They missed only one turn. Soon they found the small room. The lounge had a microwave oven and small galley. It was also equipped with four televisions, one mounted near the ceiling in each of the corners of the room.

One television was tuned to C-SPAN. It showed live footage of the debate going in the United States Senate. A second television showed the United Nations General Assembly—still in session after twelve hours. The third screen showed the Japanese Diet—also in session after many hours.

A fourth TV was tuned to INN. Brian was certain this was a polite gesture for their benefit. Max Hulse was droning on about the defensive measures the Japanese Navy would employ against Godzilla.

Nick found a remote control and switched channels on the fourth screen. It showed a patch of water, lit redly by infrared scopes. The picture was jerky, but at the center of the screen, Godzilla was clearly visible. The creature was walking on the bottom of the Sea of Japan—only his head and neck projected from the water.

"That's a live feed from one of the patrol ships pacing Godzilla," Lieutenant Takado said, entering the room. She went over to the galley and poured a cup of green tea. "Would you like some?" she asked politely.

"*Domo,*" Yoshi said with a smile.

Soon everyone had taken a seat around the table. They sipped tea and watched the monitors. Occasionally, Nick would change the sound—turning down the volume on one TV, and turning up another.

"The governments of Iran, Iraq, Libya, and Syria

have just issued a joint statement," the CNN anchor-woman said somberly. "It reads in part: Godzilla is a Sword of Allah. It is a weapon to punish the decadent western democracies and the people of Japan. Any aggression against Godzilla will be considered an act of terrorism against the nations of Islam.

"In other news, the North Korean delegation has walked out of UN talks. They object to U.S. warships sailing close to their shores.

"Meanwhile, a spokesman for Greenpeace demanded that the creature called Godzilla be designated an endangered species and protected under international environmental protection laws similar to those enacted to save the whales—"

"The world has forgotten the horrors of the past!" Yoshi suddenly shouted, his fist crashing on the table.

Brian was shocked by the Japanese youth's emotional outburst. As long as he'd known him, Yoshi had been quiet and reserved. He wasn't the excitable type.

"Whoa, Yoshi!" Nick cried. "Calm down, man."

"People today are crazy," Yoshi continued. "They are so…so *ignorant!*"

"They *do* fiddle while Rome burns," Nick agreed. "But people have always been that way."

"Have they?" Admiral Willis said as he entered the room.

Lieutenant Takado jumped to attention.

Admiral Willis waved her back to her chair. "We'll have no more of *that,* Lieutenant," he said with a drawl. "For the duration of this crisis, I'm your commanding officer, but all this salutin's gotta go."

There was an obvious twinkle in Uncle Maxwell's eyes, but only Brian could see it.

"Yes, sir," Lieutenant Takado said, still standing at attention. Brian smiled. Obviously, she wasn't accustomed to the laid-back style of the Texas military man.

"I guess you've been watching television," the admiral said with a sigh. "The United Nations seems to be paralyzed—as usual. But the political aspect of the current crisis no longer concerns us. We've run out of time."

He scanned their faces. "Godzilla is changing direction and beginning to head for land. If he continues on his present course, he will come ashore on the main island of Honshu—perhaps near the city of Hamada…"

Yoshi gasped. Lieutenant Takado's face remained rigid, but her jaws tensed.

"The Russians, the Chinese, the British, and even the French are with us," the admiral continued. "At dawn, United States Air Force F-15 Strike Eagles from Osan Air Force Base in Korea will attack Godzilla from the air. This attack will be followed with an assault by warships of the Japanese Maritime Self-Defense Force. In short, tomorrow we hit Godzilla with everything we've got. And may God help us all."

Nick whistled. Yoshi smiled triumphantly. Brian felt a little sick. *Maybe I just don't have my sea legs yet,* he told himself.

The admiral scanned the faces in the room.

"Get your sleep," he ordered them sternly. "Tomorrow is your baptism by fire…"

CHAPTER 11

INTO THE FIRE!

May 31, 1998, 4:05 A.M.
Osan Air Force Base, South Korea

Captain Paul "the Gipper" Reagan—no relation to
the former president of the United States—eased
back on the throttle of his F-15E Strike Eagle. The
twin-engine fighter/bomber was fast and sleek in
the air, but down on the tarmac it almost seemed
to waddle. The smart bombs that hung from both
wings, and the huge fuel tanks, which were filled
to capacity, weighted the aircraft down.

It was a bumpy ride as Captain Reagan slid in
behind the next aircraft on the flight line. Easing
the throttle back even farther, he "parked" his aircraft behind the two in front of him.

"How does everything check?" he asked his
weapons systems officer, who sat in the cockpit
behind him.

"Just fine, captain," Captain Jennifer "Doris" Day
said into the microphone. "The link to the global
positioning system is up and running, so I know
where we're going. Weapons systems are a go."

Just then a familiar voice crackled into his earphones.

"Nice rudder, Doris!" Captain Jackson "T-Bone" Boudreau said from Stalker Four, the aircraft that eased into position behind them. Captain Reagan couldn't help but snicker.

"Yeah, Stalker Three," Boudreau's backseater, Juan "Tony" Orlando, chimed in. "That's a *real* nice rudder."

Captain Reagan heard his backseater sigh. "Adolescents!" she said. "Stop looking up my afterburners!"

Captain Day was one the first female weapons systems officers—or wizzos—in the squadron. As with any "new guy," she took a lot of ribbing—especially from Captain Boudreau, a Cajun from the bayou country of Louisiana. There were women at Osan, but most of them were pilots or technicians.

Captain Day was different. She liked to shoot—guns, bows and arrows, pool, you name it. She was particularly good at shooting smart bombs and missiles. That was why Captain Reagan's aircraft had been chosen to fly Stalker Three, and lead the second wave of the attack on Godzilla—right after Stalkers One and Two "softened up" the target.

A voice from the tower broke into their banter. The flight controller ordered them to "cut the chatter."

Captain Reagan began his third pre-flight check, just to be on the safe side.

While he worked, Reagan thought about the upcoming mission. *Fighting monsters is a lot different from fighting Iraqis,* the captain mused. *It's nothing like the Gulf War. No anti-aircraft, no fighter threat, no radar to tip the enemy off. This ought to be a milk run—but you never know.*

He recalled how he felt that night, back in 1990, when he was a rookie waiting to take off for his first combat mission over Baghdad.

"How do you feel, Doris?" he asked his backseater.

"I'd be lying if I said I wasn't nervous," she confessed. "But I know I can do the job."

I know you can, too, Reagan thought. *Or I wouldn't go up with you.*

"Speaking of which," Captain Day continued, "I'll make you a wager!"

"Oh," he replied. "And what would *that* be?"

"I'll bet you that I can hit Godzilla right in the heart—with both smart bombs!" she stated with confidence.

"Just what'll you bet?" he asked.

She thought about it for a second. "If I miss the big lizard's heart, I'll do maintenance paperwork for a month."

"Whoooo!" Captain Reagan whistled. "And what if you *don't* miss?"

"If I don't miss, you let me land this plane when we get back!"

Captain Reagan sighed. *Why do all backseaters want to be pilots?* he asked himself. "All right," he agreed finally. "But it's against regulations."

"Hey," she replied confidentially. "If I take down Godzilla, they'll wave medals in our faces when we land, not regulations."

Just then the tower came on-line again. "Stalker Flight, prepare for takeoff," the voice on the radio commanded.

*   *   *

Brian Shimura sweated in his tiny bunk aboard the *Kongo-Maru*. He turned over with a moan and threw the sheets off his body.

It's hot in here, he thought. Then he thought about it again. *No, it isn't...I'm scared.*

The revelation depressed him. Rationally, he knew he had a right to be scared. *After all, I'm nineteen years old, I'm only a student intern, and I'm going into a sea battle with a monster. Who wouldn't be scared?* he argued with himself.

But neither Yoshi nor Nick seemed afraid, he noticed. Nick was snoring away on the top bunk, and Yoshi seemed exhilarated by the whole thing. *But Yoshi's the kind of guy who wants to go to Bosnia and shoot combat footage,* Brian thought bitterly.

Why am I so afraid? he asked himself for the hundredth time. *I'm not a coward—I've surfed, skied, bungee-jumped, and even went skydiving once. It was fun. Why is this so different?*

Maybe because the whole thing is so...primal. Hunting for some freak of nature, a giant beast that could kill us all. The thought made Brian feel like some caveman, on the hunt for a dinosaur, like in that movie where Raquel Welch wore a fur loincloth.

Maybe that's it! he reasoned. *Maybe it's such a primitive, basic fear, a fear of natural terrors that still lives at the core of all of our beings.*

It's man against nature, that's what it is. But suddenly, Brian felt a chill wash over him. He shivered and pulled the sheets back over himself.

Nature almost always wins, he thought glumly. *Nature—in the guise of a bad heart—even beat my mother*. And, at that moment, he realized that there was another reason why he was so afraid. Brian had watched his mother die, and he'd learned what death really was.

When Nick, Yoshi, and Brian came on deck that morning, they were surprised by the vision that awaited them. Somehow, overnight, the *Kongo-Maru* had become surrounded by warships. Two destroyers, four frigates, and an array of support vessels steamed through the waves on either side of them. It was an impressive armada.

The day was clear and cloudless, the weather cool, and the Sea of Japan was mostly calm, with only a light chop.

When they reached the ship's bridge, Admiral Willis greeted them. Lieutenant Takado was there, wearing a combat uniform this time. Dr. Nobeyama was present, too. It was the first time any of them had seen the older man aboard the *Kongo-Maru*.

The bridge was impressive. Windows lined the front, but on either side were huge television screens feeding live pictures of the action from a dozen remote cameras. Other instruments lined the walls. Many men in white lab coats manned these monitors.

"Good morning," Admiral Willis greeted them. "Did you all have breakfast?"

They nodded their heads politely, but in truth, they had all been too nervous to eat. Nick claimed he felt seasick. Yoshi said he wanted an empty stomach to "keep the fear up." But Brian knew it was just nervousness on all of their parts.

The admiral turned and faced the monitors again. "The F-15s are about ten minutes from the target," he said. The admiral pointed out the window.

Far ahead of them, visible in the clear atmosphere, Godzilla waded across the Sea of Japan. Even at this distance, more than three miles, he was majestic. The waves lapped at his belly and upper thighs, but the rest of him was fully exposed. The monster seemed oblivious to the ships that stalked him and the helicopters that buzzed around him.

"We'll never get a better shot at Godzilla than this," the admiral said. "Unless he comes onto land, of course."

Brian, Nick, and Yoshi heard the blast of a ship's horn from the largest of the warships. The Japanese fleet sped up. Soon the ships were pulling ahead of the *Kongo-Maru*. The navy was preparing to outflank Godzilla.

"We'll hang back here," the admiral told them. "But when the fighting starts, we'll switch to hydrofoil and circle around the battle." He pointed to the television monitors on both sides of the bridge. They showed images of Godzilla from various angles.

"There are dozens of remote cameras," he said. "The cameras are mounted on helicopters, ships, small patrol craft—even high above in AWACs aircraft. Everything is being fed to us and recorded." The admiral couldn't hide the excitement in his voice.

Dr. Nobeyama, too, looked eager for the action to begin. "We'll learn more about Godzilla today than we have in the last forty years," the Japanese scientist remarked with enthusiasm.

Yoshi tapped Brian on the shoulder. "I'm going topside," he said, "to set up my camera on the super-structure." He turned swiftly and left the bridge.

As Yoshi departed, he passed a tall Japanese man with a shaven head and tattoos running up both muscular arms. This man stepped onto the bridge. Brian noticed that the stranger had cold eyes, and his mouth was stretched into a grim frown. Admiral Willis turned and spoke to the tattooed man in fluent Japanese.

Brian touched Lieutenant Takado's arm. "Who's that?" he asked, pointing to the man.

"That's Buntaro," she answered. "He's a har-pooner from the Japanese whaling fleet. If the air-craft and ships fail to destroy Godzilla, then we will have to get close enough to fire the trident har-poon into the creature's body.

"Buntaro is an expert marksman," she continued. "He will fire that harpoon from the gun on the bow."

"I want to go on deck with him," Brian said, sud-denly making up his mind. "I mean, if it comes to that…"

"I do not think that Admiral Willis would approve. It will be very dangerous," Lieutenant Takado objected. "We will be very close to Godzilla."

"If the monster decides to destroy this vessel, it won't matter if I'm on deck or hiding in my bunk. We'll all die just the same. And anyway, my uncle dragged me out here—he can't object if I actually *do* something!"

"Hai," she answered, admiring his bravery. "That is quite true. But I'm still not sure—"

"I'm going," Brian repeated. Lieutenant Takado heard the determination in his voice loud and clear.

"Admiral!" one of the crewmen shouted from the radar station. "The helicopters are clearing out to give the fighters room....Yes! We have F-15s incoming."

"Stalker One to Stalker Three, come in."

Captain Reagan heard the call over his earphones. It was from one of the two aircraft that would lead the attack. He keyed his mike and responded. "This is Stalker Three, over."

"We see the target ahead, Stalker Three," the voice replied. "We're going in with machine guns... just to test the water."

"Be careful, Stalker One and Two," Captain Reagan said. "Come out of the sun if at all possible. Hopefully the creature will be blinded by the glare."

"Roger, Stalker Three," the voice acknowledged. And then Captain Reagan heard the pilot cry, "Here we go!" over the radio. The first two F-15s broke formation and dived toward the monster far below.

Two F-15s streaked out of the sky and flashed over the *Kongo-Maru*. The sound of their twin jet engines was deafening. From his vantage point on top of the bridge, Yoshi covered his ears. On the bridge, Nick whooped. "Go get 'em, boys!"

As Stalkers One and Two neared Godzilla, the monster's head filled their sights.

"Fire!" the pilot of Stalker One commanded. Both aircraft opened up with their M61A1 Vulcan 20mm minicannons, mounted on the right side of the fuselage. The guns rained hot lead onto the target.

Bright yellow explosions erupted all over Godzilla's face, chest, and neck. They looked tiny against the creature's vast bulk. For almost five seconds, the F-15s poured bullets into Godzilla, until their shells were depleted.

"Break off!" the lead pilot cried into his mike. In a graceful maneuver, the aircraft separated. They both flew past Godzilla at eye level, on either side of the creature's massive head.

Godzilla howled in rage and confusion. With a speed that belied his size, Godzilla's head turned. He followed one of the F-15s—Stalker Two—with his cold, reptilian gaze.

Blue lightning danced up and down Godzilla's dorsal spikes. The monster opened his mouth, revealing twin rows of sharp, ragged teeth. A blast of blue-white fire shot out of Godzilla's mouth. The beam reached out toward Stalker Two and just brushed its wing.

The whole airplane shuddered. The pilot jinked the aircraft to one side, pulling it away from the monster's blast. When his fighter was out of harm's way, the pilot examined the wing. Paint was burned away, and some of the metal was scorched and even melted in spots.

"Wow! That was *too* close," cried the pilot of Stalker Two.

Captain Reagan heard the alarm in the other pilot's voice. "Is everything all right, Stalker Two?"

The pilot, regaining his composure, answered immediately. "Everything's okay, sir. But that was a close one. Be advised, Godzilla can shoot back!"

As the fighter pulled away from Godzilla, the wizzo aboard Stalker Two spoke. "What was it that General McConnell asked us to do during the attack?" he asked over the radio.

Captain Reagan smiled behind his oxygen mask. "He wanted us to observe Godzilla's visual acuity," he replied.

"Well," Stalker Two's wizzo answered back, "I don't know about his visual acuity—but his aim is pretty damn good!"

There was nervous laughter from the rest of the squadron.

"Okay, folks," Captain Reagan said, taking a deep breath. "It's back to business. Let's line up for the first bombing run. All set, Doris?"

"Ready, captain," she replied crisply from behind him. "Target in sight."

"Break right!" Captain Reagan shouted, putting the F-15 into a steep dive. T-Bone, piloting Stalker Four, was right by his side.

"Those cannons didn't even *dent* Godzilla!" Nick said in amazement. Dr. Nobeyama nodded, his eyes glued to one of the instrument panels. "It is as we feared, Admiral," the old man said cryptically.

"Let's not jump to conclusions, Doctor. We'll just see how the smart bombs do," the admiral replied. Though his words were hopeful, Admiral Willis's expression was grim.

*   *   *

"Keep it tight, Stalker Four," Captain Reagan said into his mike. "Just pickle your bombs and pull up, T-Bone. Remember that this S.O.B. can shoot back!"

"Roger," the Cajun answered tersely.

"How's it look, Doris?" Captain Reagan asked his wizzo.

"Just keep her steady," she replied. "I got that lizard on my screen."

Stalkers Three and Four raced over the water at less than two hundred feet above the waves. Turbulence rising from the Sea of Japan buffeted the aircraft. But Captain Day kept the creature centered in her sights.

"Bombs away!" she cried. Two GBUs—Guided Bomb Units—leaped off the wings and streaked toward Godzilla at the speed of sound. To his right, out of the corner of his eyes, Captain Reagan saw two bombs drop from Stalker Four as well. As the guided bombs rushed toward their target, Captain Reagan squinted his eyes in anticipation of their explosive impact.

One...two...three...four! All four GBUs hit Godzilla. Captain Day whooped into Reagan's ear. "Dead on!" she cried. "Two to the heart."

A yellow plume of fire, then a second, and a third, engulfed Godzilla completely. The last bomb, from Stalker Four, bounced off the monster's shoulder and detonated harmlessly over the water. Red-orange fire filled Captain Reagan's vision.

"Break off!" he commanded. *If it's still standing after that, then the S.O.B. can't be killed,* the captain told himself.

Stalkers Three and Four split up, each flying through the smoke and fire past the monster's head. In the center of the smoke, Godzilla remained standing.

The monster turned his feral head. Faster than anyone would have believed, his eyes narrowed as he focused on one of the objects that had stung him. Again, blue lightning danced down his dorsal spikes and a jet of blue-white fire burst from his mouth.

As Stalker Three rushed over Godzilla and rose back up into the blue morning sky, Captain Reagan saw a flash of light to his right. Over his headphones he heard terrible screams of pain and terror...and then nothing. He turned his head in time to see Stalker Four disappear in a ball of orange fire and black smoke. The fireball arced down toward the Sea of Japan.

"Oh my God," Captain Day moaned. "T-Bone! Tony!"

With a sinking feeling in the pit of his stomach, Captain Reagan watched the burning mass that was Stalker Four plunge into the Sea of Japan far below.

He saw no parachutes.

CHAPTER 12

WAR AT SEA

May 31, 1998, 7:01 A.M.
Somewhere in the Sea of Japan

Less than ten minutes after they first launched their futile attack, the F-15s from Osan Air Base broke off and returned to base. They were low on fuel and out of bombs and ammunition.

Nothing they had launched or shot at Godzilla had seemed to affect the monster. Instead, two F-15s had been lost—one from the second wave and one from the fourth. Their crews were lying at the bottom of the Sea of Japan.

Admiral Willis turned away from the windows.

"It's time for the Japanese Navy to give it a try," he said, his lips tight.

"Sir!" the man on watch called out. "The warships are moving to attack position." Far ahead of the *Kongo-Maru*, the navy ships were maneuvering for the attack.

"And so will we. Go to hydrofoil," the admiral commanded.

The hydrofoil leaped ahead in the water. As the *Kongo-Maru* picked up speed, Admiral Willis locked eyes with Buntaro. The muscular Japanese smiled thinly and bowed to the admiral.

Soon the hydrofoil was streaking across the Sea of Japan at over seventy miles an hour. Buntaro turned and left the bridge.

Unnoticed by everyone but Lieutenant Takado, Brian followed the harpooner into the bowels of the *Kongo-Maru.*

The lieutenant hurried after the two, catching up with Brian in a long corridor that led to the bow. "Stop, Brian...please," she cried, grabbing his arm. "You must not do this!"

"I have to do it," Brian insisted, yanking his arm free.

"But you are a reporter, not a soldier!" she argued.

"So I gotta find something to report, then, don't I?" he said. "Nick's a science correspondent, he's got the bridge covered. Yoshi's a cameraman. But I'm nothing but a sportscaster-wannabe—unless I *do* something!" he cried. "I've got to do something!"

Emiko saw the raw fear in Brian's young face, but she also saw his determination to defeat that fear. She hesitated. Brian turned and ran after the harpooner.

As he rounded the next corner, Brian saw the man climbing up a ladder to an open hatch. Brian followed without hesitation. At the top of the ladder, he poked his head out of the hatchway. Brian was immediately buffeted by the winds that swept across the bow. The *Kongo-Maru* was skimming across the waves at a tremendous speed, making a long arc that would bring it around behind Godzilla.

* * *

"The American airplanes have failed," said Admiral Toyohashi to the officers assembled on the bridge of the task force flagship, the destroyer *Hatsuyuki*. He scanned their eager faces, then issued his order to attack. "Prepare to launch Godzilla Counter-measure Plan B!"

"Banzai!" the officers cried as one, then hurried off to perform their duties. The *Hatsuyuki* was to lead the attack against Godzilla, and the admiral's chest swelled with pride at the honor the emperor granted him.

Klaxons blared all over the ship as the crew manned combat positions. The six warships sliced through the water, leaving the support vessels behind.

From the helipad of the *Hatsuyuki*'s sister ship, the destroyer *Kurama,* three heavily armed SH-60 Seahawk helicopters lifted into the sky. These five-bladed, twin-engine choppers, outfitted with Vulcan miniguns, missiles, and flare launchers, were meant to confuse Godzilla by launching a barrage of munitions at his face and head.

Admiral Toyohashi knew that if Godzilla could blast a speeding jet out of the sky, he could easily hit one of these ships. Toyohashi hoped that the helicopters' flares would temporary blind—or at least confuse—Godzilla.

As the two destroyers, and the frigates *Chikugo*, *Iwase*, *Yoshino*, and *Chitose* closed in on the monster, Godzilla turned and faced the approaching vessels.

"Weapons systems ready!" an ensign cried. Admiral Toyohashi nodded. He strode across the bridge and peered through the bulletproof windows.

"Launch the attack!" the admiral commanded.

A second later, the 127mm deck guns, mounted in turrets on the destroyers' bows, opened up. The sound was deafening. Anti-aircraft guns began firing, too, pouring steel-jacketed shells onto the target.

As hundreds of tons of munitions hit his massive body, Godzilla lifted his head and howled in rage. His mighty tail thrashed, churning up the ocean in its wake. His eyes flashed angrily, and his lips curled back to reveal his six-foot-long teeth.

Pressing the attack, the Seahawk helicopters buzzed around Godzilla's head, firing flares, missiles, and bullets at the creature's face. Godzilla lifted his arms and blinked his eyes in a vain attempt to ward off the blinding pyrotechnics.

Admiral Toyohashi smiled. *We are winning,* he told himself. *Today Gojira dies!*

The monster's ear-shattering roar could be heard over the sound of the guns. As the task force moved within range of Godzilla's terrible radioactive fire, the ships slipped off into two lines. Each row of ships had a frigate in the lead, followed by a destroyer and another frigate. Admiral Toyohashi's ship, the *Hatsuyuki,* took the right flank.

In minutes, Godzilla was surrounded by warships, which kept pounding the creature with tons of high explosives, shrapnel, and armor-piercing shells.

The *Kongo-Maru* sped rapidly past the battle,

warily circling the monstrous creature and the ships that assaulted it.

Clinging to a hatch, Brian watched as Buntaro prepared the harpoon. The gun itself was precariously mounted on a platform that extended forward well past the tip of the bow. A narrow railed catwalk was the only way to get to the gun.

The harpooner had spotted Brian when he first climbed onto the deck, but ignored the youth and immediately returned to his task. For a few minutes, Buntaro ran back and forth along a narrow catwalk that led to the hydraulic harpoon gun. He adjusted instruments and activated the weapon's range-finding guidance system.

As the hydrofoil finished circling the battle and approached Godzilla from behind, Buntaro drew a trident-shaped harpoon out of a metal box welded to the hull. Then he tilted the gun upward and carefully slid the harpoon down inside the barrel.

Next, the harpooner pulled one end of a fiber-optic cable out of a winch mounted on the side of the bow. He attached the thin cable to a socket on the harpoon. Then Buntaro shouldered the weapon and peered through the sight.

Brian heard louder explosions. He looked past the tattooed harpooner and could see Godzilla's back, where blue fire danced and played along the three rows of bony spikes. His tail was flailing, stirring up the sea in the path of the oncoming Japanese fleet.

The hydrofoil was getting close to Godzilla now...very, very close.

* * *

Admiral Toyohashi watched with admiration as his ships maneuvered around the creature. On the left flank, the frigate *Iwase* led the way. As the warship drew closer to Godzilla, it launched a half-dozen Mark 68 anti-submarine torpedoes from tubes mounted on its side.

The torpedoes streaked toward their target, leaving a white trail of bubbles in their wake as they shot through the water. In less than a minute, all six torpedoes struck Godzilla's submerged legs and tail.

The explosions blasted huge geysers of water hundreds of feet into the air. The monster shuddered and howled again, but he remained standing.

Godzilla turned toward the source of the irritant—the frigate *Iwase*.

Familiar blue lightning arced up Godzilla's dorsal spines. The monster opened his mouth and a hot jet of radioactive fire spewed forth. Fortunately, the blast that burst from his throat was undirected, but he did manage to scatter the three Seahawk choppers buzzing around his face.

With Godzilla's vision cleared for the first time since the sea attack began, the nuclear giant turned and focused his reptilian gaze on the *Iwase*, which had already sped past. The monster's spikes lit up with blue flashes, and Godzilla fired his ray once again.

This time his aim was better.

The glowing blast played across the *Iwase*'s superstructure. Sailors on deck were instantly vaporized. In another second, the steel deck plates began to melt. The forward gun turret exploded first, its munitions ignited by the terrible heat.

Then the ocean was rocked as a second blast tore the whole superstructure off the hull and flung it high into the air. Five more explosions followed, each one sending geysers of fire and smoke into the blue morning sky.

The *Iwase*'s hull, which was transformed into a funeral pyre for the unfortunate crew, surged ahead for a few moments more. Then the ship capsized and sank, dragging 167 souls to the bottom of the sea.

"Break off the attack!" Admiral Toyohashi cried. His command was instantly radioed to the entire fleet.

But the monster was moving with a sudden speed that belied its immense size. Just as Toyohashi's destroyer steamed past Godzilla, the creature slammed his mammoth body against the ship.

Admiral Toyohashi and the other bridge officers were thrown from their feet as the ship tilted precariously. Fire alarms were cut off and the bridge lights went out. There was darkness for a moment until the battery-powered emergency lights came on. Now the bridge was illuminated with an eerie red glow.

The admiral struggled to his feet. His head was bleeding from a cut sustained when he hit an electronics console.

"Full speed ahead!" he cried. "Take us out of here!"

"Sir!" the first officer cried. "The engines are damaged and the hull is breached. We are taking on water."

Outside, Godzilla grappled with the destroyer

like a giant sumo wrestler. The creature used his clawed fists to batter whole sections of the superstructure flat. On the bridge, over the sound of the guns, terrified screams could be heard.

As the *Hatsuyuki* shuddered under the pummeling, the radioman cried out. "Admiral! The other ships are moving to our assistance."

"No!" the admiral replied. *There will be no more loss of life,* he decided. "Tell them to break off the attack and get as far away from the creature as possible."

The radioman nodded and sent out the command. The destroyer shuddered again, and the fire alarms blared. Godzilla's roar echoed throughout the doomed ship.

"Damage report!" the admiral cried.

"Fire below deck!" the first officer said as he gripped the controls.

Admiral Toyohashi stumbled to the bulletproof windows. He looked up at Godzilla. At that moment, the creature stepped back from the *Hatsuyuki* and stared down at the crippled ship with a predatory gaze. Blue lightning flashed, and Godzilla opened its mouth.

It's karma, Admiral Toyohashi thought. *We can do no more.*

Brian watched as the *Hatsuyuki* exploded. The ship was lifted out of the water by the blast, and then split into two pieces. The stern sank instantly. The front half of the ship turned over on its side. Brian could see sailors leaping off the *Hatsuyuki*'s deck and into the Sea of Japan.

His enemy defeated, Godzilla turned away from the wreckage. With a triumphant howl, he continued forward.

Following the admiral's final command, the rest of the Japanese fleet was giving Godzilla a wide berth. *We should try to rescue some of the survivors!* Brian thought when he realized that the other ships were nowhere near the men in the water. But the *Kongo-Maru* did not alter its course. It still approached Godzilla from behind.

In the air above its head, the Seahawk helicopters continued to fire flares and munitions into Godzilla's eyes in an attempt to cover the fleet's retreat.

Suddenly, the *Kongo-Maru* turned. Brian lost his precarious grip on the hatch and almost fell into the Sea of Japan when the hydrofoil jinked to one side, then another, in an attempt to get past Godzilla's thrashing tail.

A smell burned Brian's nose. It was a combination of cordite, gunpowder, ozone, and wet fish. They were close enough to Godzilla to smell the beast, Brian realized. Fortunately, the creature seemed oblivious to the *Kongo-Maru*'s rapid approach.

On the catwalk, Buntaro pointed the harpoon at the back of Godzilla's neck—a target almost two hundred feet above the waves. Brian grabbed the railing and climbed onto the catwalk, too. He slowly edged his way toward the harpoon station.

I want to see this, he thought with determination. *I want to have something to report—that's my job.*

*   *   *

Two hundred feet above the ocean, one of the Seahawk helicopters got too close to Godzilla.

The monster flailed its arm and backhanded the aircraft. The Seahawk's tail rotor was ripped loose, and the pilot lost all control. The helicopter flipped over Godzilla's shoulder and slammed into a row of dorsal spines. Then the Seahawk, its main engines still turning the five-bladed rotors, bounced and rolled down Godzilla's broad back.

The *Kongo-Maru,* which had just dodged Godzilla's thrashing tail, streaked right into the path of the falling helicopter. Brian watched in horror as the mangled machine dropped toward the very deck he was standing on. Time seemed to slow down.

"Buntaro! Look out!" Brian cried over the noise and chaos. The harpooner, who was preparing to shoot, took his eyes away from the scope on the harpoon gun. He saw the rotors spinning toward him.

And he froze.

Brian hit the deck just as the helicopter crashed into the sea off their starboard bow. The fuselage missed the *Kongo-Maru* by mere inches. But the rotors did the damage. As Brian watched helplessly, five whirling blades cut through the deck, shattered the catwalk, and struck the paralyzed harpooner.

Buntaro disappeared in a red mist.

The whole vessel shuddered. Then the rotors caught for an instant. The helicopter's fuselage slammed against the hull as the ship dragged the shattered remains for a few yards before the twisted wreckage finally broke loose.

Still clinging to the deck, Brian could smell kerosene. Fuel from the helicopter was splattered all over the bow. He also saw blood and bits of cloth—all that remained of Buntaro.

Then he looked up. The hydrofoil was almost past Godzilla's tail. He knew what he had to do.

Scrambling to his feet, Brian climbed over the twisted debris of the wrecked catwalk. He reached the harpoon, which seemed to be intact despite the accident. Brian spotted a headphone/microphone set resting in a cradle. He put it on.

"Uncle Maxwell," he cried into the microphone. "Can you hear me?"

Up on the bridge, Admiral Willis and Nick had watched as the chopper took Buntaro's life. Then they watched as an unidentifiable figure ran across the deck and took the dead harpooner's station. The radio speaker above their heads crackled to life.

"Uncle Maxwell!" the voice cried. "Can you hear me?"

Nick's eyes widened. "That's Brian!" He turned and saw Lieutenant Takado standing in the doorway. Their eyes met, and then she looked away guiltily.

"Brian, what the—what are you doing out there?" Admiral Willis barked over the radio.

Unfortunately, Brian's radio receiver had been damaged in the wreck. Brian knew he was listening to his uncle's voice, but the words were almost unintelligible.

"I can't hear you," Brian replied. "But *keep circling Godzilla*...I'm sure I can fire this thing!" He grabbed the handle and elevated the harpoon. He tried to look through the sight, but there was a streak of red on the lens, blocking his vision. Shivering, Brian wiped the blood away.

Godzilla's back loomed in the gunsight.

"Brian, you have to hit Godzilla in the neck, repeat, th…ck." His uncle's voice crackled in his ear. "Don't for…to release th…ty, remem… rel…saf…" Brian ignored the garbled command and squeezed the trigger.

Nothing happened.

Then the voice crackled into his ears again. "You have t…release…safety…" Brian looked at the harpoon. Of course—the safety switch! He located the button and depressed it. A red light on the base of the harpoon gun lit up, showing the weapon was armed and ready.

Again Brian peered through the sight. He was still on target. Brian held his breath and squeezed the trigger.

The harpoon left the barrel with a loud whoosh. To Brian's surprise, the gun had a powerful kick that slammed into his shoulder. Brian ignored the pain. He watched as the harpoon arced into the air.

It struck Godzilla right at the base of the neck, near the spinal column. The long, fiber-optic cable whistled through the winch and was strung along behind. When the harpoon hit flesh, smaller anchors, like super-sharp fishhooks, embedded themselves into Godzilla's hide. The monster was so huge, its skin so thick, that it didn't even notice the harpoon striking its flesh.

Brian heard whoops of triumph over his headset. Suddenly exhausted, he slumped to the deck and started to shake uncontrollably. He still gripped the handle of the harpoon gun as the *Kongo-Maru* stopped circling the monster and took up a position behind it.

Brian was still slumped there—cold, wet, and shivering—when Lieutenant Takado and Nick came out onto the fuel-soaked deck to get him.

CHAPTER 13

GODZILLA 101

May 31, 1998, 3:55 P.M.
Aboard the Kongo-Maru
Somewhere in the Sea of Japan

Brian showered, rested, and dressed in fresh clothes before he stepped into the lounge of the *Kongo-Maru*.

The tiny room was empty. He boiled some water at the kitchenette and made green tea and an instant noodle pack he selected from the shelf. As he ate, Brian recalled his uncle's reaction to his stunt. He smiled at the memory.

When Brian had been dragged back into the ship, stinking of fuel and held up on his feet by Nick and Lieutenant Takado, it was a stern-faced officer of the U.S. Navy high command who greeted him.

"Just what do you think you were *doing* out there?" Admiral Willis barked angrily. "You could have been killed, boy! Just what was I supposed to tell your family? That I took their oldest son fishing—for Godzilla!?"

Brian was too weak, and too numb, to respond.

But he smiled at his uncle—which *really* made the admiral mad!

Admiral Willis put his beefy hands on his hips. "And *don't* give me that smart-assed grin of yours, either! I'd tear your head off except for one thing—you did *good!*"

Then the admiral's craggy features broke into a smile. "Yes, you heard me. You did good.

"I'm happy to say we're getting solid data through the cable," he informed them all. "The *Kongo-Maru* will follow Godzilla until he submerges too deep for our cable to reach, or until the cable is broken for some other reason. Every second that cable is feeding us information is precious. We're learning about Godzilla, troops!"

The admiral paused again. Then he slapped his nephew on the back. "Congratulations, son," he said. "I'm proud of you. And I'm sure your father will be proud of you, too."

With that, the admiral turned and headed back to the bridge.

Brian finished his noodle pack and tossed the cup into the garbage bin. Then he picked up the remote and switched on one of the televisions.

This monitor was tuned to CNN, where an attractive anchorwoman was updating world financial news.

"...Word of the tragic attack and the Japanese Navy's failure to stop Godzilla has the financial markets of the world—which were already jittery—near panic. The Japanese stock market is in meltdown. The Nikkei average has plunged almost twenty percent since noon, Tokyo time. The yen is also down against the dollar and the pound.

"There is fear that the economic panic will spread to other financial markets when the New York and London stock markets open in the morning. In other news—"

Brian turned it off. *I've heard enough.*

At that moment, Nick entered the lounge.

"Hey, if it isn't our international star!" he quipped.

"Huh?" Brian replied.

"Our pal Yoshi—the eye behind the camera who never misses a shot—was filming the attack from the top of the bridge," Nick informed Brian. "He's got the whole battle on tape: the destruction of both ships, the helicopter crash...everything!"

Brian swallowed hard. "Everything?" he asked weakly.

"Yup!" Nick beamed. "Including your little stint as a harpooner. Yoshi sent those pictures back to INN through a satellite uplink.

"Your homage to *Moby-Dick* has been broadcast worldwide on INN. You're a *star,* son!"

Brian's mouth dropped open. Then he actually giggled. He began to laugh uncontrollably. Soon, Nick joined in. Their laughter echoed throughout the ship.

Lieutenant Takado and Yoshi were passing through the hallway. They peeked in, exchanged puzzled glances, and left again, unnoticed by the laughing duo.

For Brian, the laughter washed away the terrible tensions of the day. When he was finally finished, he rubbed his tired eyes. He discovered that he actually felt better.

"How *do* you feel, old man?" Nick asked when they calmed down.

"Not bad for someone who was in a sea battle, a helicopter crash, and a close encounter with Godzilla, and gained international stardom—and all before noon!"

"Well," Nick said, "you've got to admit it's more exciting than covering the Winter Olympics." They laughed some more.

"So" Brian said, sighing. "Yoshi got it all on tape, did he? *And* he sent it back to headquarters..."

"He did," Nick nodded. "He'll probably win an Emmy."

"It'll be awarded posthumously," Brian said. "'Cause I'm gonna kill him."

He's aged a decade since this morning, Brian thought when Dr. Nobeyama entered the crowded lounge two hours later. The Japanese scientist was tense with anxiety, and the weight of the world seemed to be on his stooped shoulders.

The old man nodded to the assembled officers and technicians of the *Kongo-Maru*. They were packed into the lounge, along with Nick and Brian. Everyone was anxious to hear what Dr. Nobeyama's experiments had revealed.

The Japanese scientist took a seat at the head of the table. Admiral Willis stood at the old man's shoulder. His face, too, was grim.

Lieutenant Takado entered last, carrying a video-cassette. She slipped a tape into the VCR and pressed PLAY. Instantly the four television screens were filled with an image of Godzilla, taken just that morning. She froze the picture, turned to the assembly, and spoke.

"Before Dr. Nobeyama speaks, I've been asked to give you an update on the battle—and on Godzilla's movements," she said in English. Though most of the technicians present were Japanese, some were from other countries. English was the scientific team's language of choice.

"Four American airmen were lost in the initial air attack," Lieutenant Takado said grimly. "Two Japanese ships were lost with almost no survivors—there are over five hundred Japanese dead, including Admiral Toyohashi, the commander."

Everyone gasped. One of the technicians—a Japanese woman who was engaged to an officer aboard the *Iwase*—began to sob. Tears rolled down her cheeks as the lieutenant continued her briefing.

"Less than an hour ago, the fiber-optic cable broke and we lost contact with the probe imbedded in Godzilla's body."

This information was greeted with disheartened moans. Lieutenant Takado pressed on.

"The good news is that over ninety percent of Dr. Nobeyama's probes, tests, and experiments were successfully performed. We managed to collect valuable data on Godzilla's physiology.

"The bad news is that Godzilla has shifted direction once again. The creature is currently moving through the Shimonoseki Straits."

Almost everyone in the room was shocked at

this bombshell. Brian gasped, too. The Shimonoseki Straits separated the Japanese island of Kyushu and the main island of Honshu.

"My God," Nick blurted out, "that will take him into the Inland Sea!"

"Yes." Lieutenant Takado nodded. "Godzilla is now moving into the most populated area of Japan." A map of Japan appeared on the television monitors. A red line traced Godzilla's possible path, through the Shimonoseki Straits and up along the Inland Sea. Lieutenant Takado continued.

"The monster will likely pass the cities of Ube, Tokuyama, Hiroshima, Kure, Okayama, Kobe, and Osaka—as well as Matsuyama and Takamatsu on the island of Shikoku. If Godzilla comes to land near any of these major cities, many thousands will perish.

"Worse still, there are dozens of nuclear power plants along the creature's route. Plants with reactors that could attract Godzilla. If the monster destroys just one of these facilities, he will feed on the radiation and grow even stronger."

Admiral Willis spoke up for the first time. "Even now, *Yuushio*-class subs of the Japanese Maritime Self-Defense Force are trackin' Godzilla. They'll serve as an early-warning system if the S.O.B. decides to come ashore."

The admiral paused. "There is, I'm sad to say, no way to stop Godzilla's progress."

"You mean that we've found no weakness to exploit?" one of the Japanese scientists asked. "No way to halt or kill the creature?"

Admiral Willis said nothing. It was Dr.

Nobeyama who replied in a quavering voice. "I am afraid that all of my theories about Godzilla have been proven," he said, shaking his head. "There is nothing humanity can do to stop Godzilla—short of vaporizing him with a nuclear weapon."

The room exploded into a babble of contentious voices. Dr. Nobeyama raised his quaking hand and called for silence. "Please look at the television monitors," the old man said when everyone calmed down. "Watch the tape we have prepared."

All eyes turned to the screen. The map disappeared, to be replaced by an image of Godzilla. The picture showed the monster facing the camera as he moved ponderously through the Sea of Japan.

"The creature's bones are denser that titanium steel—they are perhaps the hardest material in the universe, capable of carrying his entire weight without shattering." The picture froze. A computer-generated image of internal organs was superimposed over Godzilla's body.

"Godzilla is, of course, highly radioactive. But the amazing thing is that the creature somehow controls the amount of radiation he gives off," Dr. Nobeyama continued, his voice gaining strength.

"When Godzilla is angry or threatened, he gives off increasing amounts of intense radiation. This energy surge is climaxed by the ray that he fires through his mouth. The creature has a heart, lungs, a stomach...but he also has this..."

A red pointer appeared on the tape, highlighting a strange bundle of tissue between the heart, lungs, and stomach.

"This organ acts much like a nuclear reactor," the aged scientist said. "Radioactivity is generated there in much the same way as it is generated in a nuclear reactor. This organ is connected to the lungs, and is the origin of Godzilla's destructive ray."

More startled voices were heard. Brian looked at Nick, who seemed stunned at the revelation.

"As amazing as all this seems, it pales beside our next discovery." Dr. Nobeyama paused. Lieutenant Takado handed him a cup of green tea. He drank, then set the cup down slowly.

"Please look at the monitors," he said.

The image had changed. Now Godzilla could be seen taking hits from the guns of the Japanese fleet. Explosions erupted at various points on the creature's arms, torso, and legs. The picture focused on a small section at the base of Godzilla's neck. As that portion of the creature expanded to fill the screen, a shell struck it, exploding.

Suddenly, the picture went into reverse, then forward again, but at very slow motion. "When this 127mm shell from the *Iwase* struck Godzilla, it caused a massive wound—look." The picture froze again.

Yes, Brian thought. *I can see it.* And so could everyone else.

When the shell detonated against the monster's body, there was a fountain of blood, and gouts of flesh were blasted from Godzilla's neck. But before the smoke cleared, the wound was gone—healed completely—as if it had never been inflicted.

"Godzilla's greatest defensive weapon is his

amazing regenerative powers," explained Dr. Nobeyama. "The radiation that created Godzilla also mutated the creature's molecular structure. Whatever damage our weapons can cause actually heals in microseconds."

Admiral Willis suddenly spoke up. "That means that nothing in our arsenal—short of a nuclear bomb—can destroy Godzilla."

Dr. Nobeyama nodded, then spoke again. "Godzilla is capable of complete regeneration of damaged tissue instantaneously. It seems that my theory was correct—Godzilla cannot be killed unless he is completely disintegrated."

The old man slammed his fist against the table in a rare display of emotion. *"If the authorities had listened to me, then all those men would not have died!"* he cried, anguish in his voice.

It was Nick who spoke first. "You mean you told the military that Godzilla was capable of this... regeneration?"

The old man looked at Nick and nodded.

"Then the Japanese and American military sent those men to die for nothing," Nick said, his voice rising. "They *knew* all along that their weapons wouldn't work!"

"Hold on, boy," Admiral Willis interrupted. "Don't jump to conclusions. Before today, all this was a *theory*. Neither Dr. Nobeyama nor I had any *proof!*"

"Well, you have it now," Nick replied. "So what are you going to do to stop Godzilla?"

Neither Dr. Nobeyama nor Admiral Willis answered his question.

CHAPTER 14

LANDFALL!

June 6, 1998, 5:23 A.M.
Onomichi, a small town on the San-yo plain
The Japanese island of Honshu

"Where is Ken?" Goro asked yet again, slapping his pudgy arms on his shoulders for warmth. "He promised us some hot tea!"

"He's coming, don't worry," Shiro said, throwing another sliver of charcoal into the tiny metal stove that provided scant warmth. "And anyway," Shiro added, "with all that fat, *you* should be warm, at least!"

"Bah," Goro spat. He gripped the edge of the stone wall and looked over. His eyes followed the trail that led up, through the woods, to the town's century-old tower.

"Ken's not even on the trail yet!" Goro whined. "By the time he gets back with our tea, it'll be time to go home."

"This cold is unnatural," Shiro complained, looking out across the coastline. "It's *rokugatsu—* June—and it's freezing cold this morning!"

"*Hai,*" Goro agreed with a nod. "Since Gojira has returned, the whole world is going crazy. What can you expect?"

Shiro nodded and scanned the horizon. Goro gazed through binoculars at the city and shoreline that spread out beneath them.

The tiny town of Onomichi, on the shores of Japan's Inland Sea, had been a fishing village for three centuries. But with the progress that Japan had made since World War II came industrial pollution and overfishing. The fish had mostly died out, and now fishing in the Inland Sea was illegal.

The town of Onomichi had withered.

But nine years ago, when Ohashi Motors had chosen the flat mud plain at the outskirts of Onomichi as the site of their new automobile assembly plant, everything changed. Ohashi Motors brought new jobs—and new residents—to Onomichi. Now the old town wasn't big enough to hold all the people who were moving there. The fishing pier had been transformed into a mall with fashionable shops and restaurants. Expensive pleasure craft rested in docks that once held fishing boats.

The old stone tower of Onomichi, built on the small, forested hill at the edge of the city, had once been used to watch the movements of the town's fishing fleet. Lately, it had fallen into disrepair. But that was before the coming of Godzilla.

When the people of Onomichi heard the news that Godzilla had defeated the Japanese Navy and was moving into the Inland Sea, they were thrown into a panic. The town officials held a public meeting and decided that emergency steps had to be taken.

As a precaution, the old stone tower was manned by volunteer spotters twenty-four hours a day. The tower was equipped with radios and a warning siren so the spotters could provide early warning to the villagers if Godzilla came ashore anywhere nearby.

In a burst of public-spiritedness, Shiro had volunteered to man the tower one night a week. Now, shivering in the cold, he regretted his decision.

"Oh, look at that!" Goro cried, pointing out to sea. Shiro saw it too.

"I've never seen fog move in like *that* before!" he exclaimed. "It's eerie." Goro nodded, shivering again. This time, however, it wasn't from the cold.

For the next few minutes, the two men watched in silence as tendrils of mist rolled over the town below. Soon the end of the pier, and then the shoreline, was invisible. More fog billowed in, and the entire town was slowly covered in a gray-white blanket. It was as if a cloud had fallen to earth.

"What do we do?" Goro asked. "We're spotters, but we can't see a thing!"

"We stay." Shiro shrugged. "At least until our watch is over and we are relieved."

Then they heard a tiny voice calling their names from the bottom of the tower. In the fog, it sounded very far off.

"Shiro…Goro…" the voice cried.

The two men peered into the mist, listening, but could see nothing.

"*Shiro!* I'm *lost!*" the voice cried again in audible panic.

"It's that idiot Ken!" Goro concluded finally. "He's lost in the fog." They shared a laugh.

"I'd better go down and get him," Goro said. He grabbed the flashlight and disappeared down the stone stairway.

Shiro gazed out into the fog. He shivered yet again, hoping that Goro would return quickly with Ken—and the hot tea. He listened for either of their voices, but the fog seemed to consume all sound. He could see nothing but the gray wall of fog. He felt like the only human in the world.

Shiro turned his attention to the stove. He opened the tiny door and threw in some more charcoal. He tried to warm his hands, but in the fog, the heat seemed to dissipate before it reached the tips of his fingers.

At that moment, Shiro froze. He was sure he heard a sound. It was far away…like distant thunder. He strained his ears. *Yes!* he thought. *A rumble…and it's getting closer.*

Oddly, the sound was not coming from the shore, but from inland. He turned around, his eyes vainly trying to pierce the fog. The sound grew louder.

Soon it was a steady beat—a vibration—that shook his chest. He continued to face the direction of the noise, but involuntarily took two steps backward. Now he could see a dull glow in the middle of the fog.

The glow seemed to approach him, shining through the fog eerily. As it got closer, the glow seemed to divide into two points of light, floating side by side.

Shiro was shocked to realize that the two lights were high up in the sky, even with his own line of sight. *But I'm in a tower,* he thought fearfully. He took another step back. Still the lights came forward. Closer and closer. To Shiro, they looked like two giant, gleaming eyes peering back at him from the murky haze.

"It's *Gojira!*" he screamed, falling against the desk. "The monster is here!"

Blindly, he reached out and fumbled with the radio, which was connected directly to Onomichi's only police station. Flipping the switch, he grasped the microphone. Suddenly, a powerful gust of air battered him. The wind increased, tearing at his hair and clothes. The rumbling sound grew to a roar.

While Shiro watched, open-mouthed, a Pave Low helicopter, heavy with guns, swept aside the fog. Its windows, slick with morning dew, shone like the eyes of an insect. The helicopter's twin fog lights focused on Shiro. He stood, still frozen, in the spotlights. The microphone in his hand was forgotten.

Shiro could see the pilot as he reached down and flipped a switch on his control panel. A loudspeaker outside the helicopter crackled to life.

"*Sound the alarm!*" the voice over the loudspeaker commanded. "*Godzilla has come to land...The monster is coming this way...Everyone in Onomichi must evacuate immediately!*"

Just then, Shiro's own radio came to life.

"Calling lookout tower," the voice demanded. "Answer immediately."

He lifted the mike. "Shiro here," he replied, shouting over the noise.

Even over the chopper's roar, Shiro could hear the fear and urgency in the policeman's voice. "Godzilla is coming," the policeman said. "Sound the alarm, and then get out of there." The transmission ended abruptly.

Shiro dropped the mike and pressed the alarm switch. The moan of the emergency siren swelled, deafening him. As Shiro ran to the stone stairway, the helicopter veered away from the old tower and headed down over Onomichi, its loudspeaker still blaring out the warning.

Below, the townspeople were awakened by the sound of the tower's sirens and the blare of the helicopter's loudspeaker.

"Godzilla is approaching Onomichi...Leave all your belongings and flee immediately...Evacuation routes are being established along the main highway...

"Repeat...Godzilla is approaching Onomichi."

Nick's alarm clock had just gone off when he heard the telephone ring. He answered.

"Get dressed," May McGovern's voice said briskly. "Godzilla has just come ashore."

Less than half an hour later, Nick and Brian entered the INN newsroom. It was already crowded. Yoshi was there, along with May, and he waved them both over.

As always, Nick was uncomfortable in May's presence.

"The monster has come ashore on the mainland!"Yoshi informed them both. "The Self-Defense Force is being mobilized."

"How close to Tokyo?" Nick asked.

"Very far, fortunately," Yoshi replied, pointing to the television monitor.

On the INN network, Max Hulse was reporting on Godzilla's present movements.

"Sadly," Yoshi added, "the monster's rampage is taking place at the very heart of Japan's industrial base."

The mood in the newsroom was grim, but Nick couldn't help himself—he had to make a crack about the anchorman whom he detested. It was practically a compulsion.

"Y'know, that guy makes a nuclear-powered, mutated prehistoric monster that breathes fire sound *boring*."

Brian tuned out his roommate's remark and listened to the broadcast.

"...Since Godzilla came ashore on the outskirts of Fukuyama, the monster's progress has been unopposed," the anchorman reported. "But there are now unconfirmed reports that the military is being mobilized—"

On the screen, Max Hulse paused suddenly, and touched his earphone. "I've just been told that we're getting a live feed from Blackthorn Adams and our INN camera team on the scene. Can you hear me, Blackthorn?"

The image shifted. Blackthorn Adams stood on a rooftop of an industrial building. He clutched a hand-held microphone. He wore a suit, but his tie was askew.

"I can hear you, Max," Adams replied. He looked into the camera. "I'm standing on the roof of the Ohashi Motors plant, less than half a mile from Onomichi."

The camera shifted position, away from Adams. The lens scanned the horizon, finally centering on a gray-black blob. Suddenly, the picture came into focus.

It was Godzilla! The monster was wading through a group of industrial buildings. As Brian watched, Godzilla's tail lashed out, and a factory with three huge smokestacks collapsed like a pile of dishes. Flames erupted around the monster's feet.

The image was doubly eerie because there was no sound. Then Blackthorn Adams's grim voice broke in.

"Godzilla is approaching from the south," he said. "Within moments, Ohashi Motors assembly lines number three and four will be rubble."

Again the camera image blurred, then sharpened. A telescopic shot of Godzilla's face filled the entire television screen. Brian almost jumped backward. He'd already had a few nightmares about Godzilla since that day on the *Kongo-Maru*...nightmares filled with double rows of man-sized teeth, cold, reptilian eyes, and blue radioactive fire.

"There goes the Conceptia!" Nick observed, breaking Brian's concentration.

"The what?" Brian asked.

"Ohashi Motors' answer to the Saturn," Nick replied. "That's where they built it—that pile of rubble to the left."

Just then, Everett Endicott came into the newsroom and approached the four of them.

"Come with me," he said.

"You've done well as a team so far," Endicott said when they were all seated in his executive office. "Even you, Mr. Gordon…"

Nick grinned.

"That's why I'm not happy with the network's decision." The portly news chief sighed.

Brian, Nick, Yoshi, and even May were all ears.

"The bosses back in the States want me to break you up," Endicott said. "We're stretched pretty thin here, and our coverage is suffering for it—"

There was a knock at the door. May rose and opened it. To everyone's surprise, Lieutenant Emiko Takado stepped into the room. As usual, she wore her military uniform smartly. Nick, Brian, and Yoshi greeted her warmly. After a moment, Endicott continued.

"I want Nick and Yoshi to accompany Lieutenant Takado to the front lines. Your job is to cover the upcoming battle—if there *is* one."

Yoshi smiled, anticipating more award-winning footage. Nick swallowed hard, surprised and happy with this new development. He smiled at Lieuten-ant Takado. "Traveling with Lieutenant Takado will be *my* pleasure," he said, radiating charm.

May's face remained stony.

"Brian here has brought a lot of attention to INN in the last week," Endicott stated, placing his meaty hand on Brian's shoulder. The young man's face reddened.

Since footage of the harpooning had been beamed all over the world, Brian Shimura's name had become a household word. After returning to Tokyo, Brian had given countless interviews, including a live chat with Ted Koppel on *Nightline* via satellite.

"Because of his sudden fame," Endicott continued, "the network brass wants Brian to cover the debates in the Japanese Diet, starting with Dr. Nobeyama's speech tomorrow morning.

"I hate to break up a successful team, but for now, that's the way it is. I'm sorry."

After Endicott dismissed them, the group gathered in the outer office to say their farewells.

"Take care, roomie," Nick said, slapping Brian's arm. "You won't have Lieutenant Takado here to watch your back!"

Yoshi bowed. "I will see you when we return," he said simply, and then headed for the elevators.

May and Nick did not share goodbyes. But when Nick finally departed a few minutes later, in animated conversation with the lovely Japanese military officer, May, stared daggers at the pretty lieutenant's back.

CHAPTER 15

A PLAN OF ACTION

June 7, 1998, 10:46 A.M.
The Diet building
Tokyo, Japan

The Japanese Diet members had been arguing for
over two hours. Even with the services of a first-
rate translator, Brian couldn't understand half of
what was going on. All he'd gotten out of the contentious meeting was a headache. He was bored
and disgusted—and this was only the first round of
talks!

*I guess Nick is right about one thing—politics
is the same in every country,* he thought cynically.

The main event—the speech by Dr.
Nobeyama—was already over an hour late. Brian
shifted in his seat and readjusted his earphones. In
his ear, the translator droned on. More news about
the environmental organization Greenpeace
declaring Godzilla an endangered species.

That speech was followed by a military briefing.
A general in the Japanese Self-Defense Force proposed using tank shells filled with poison or a
deadly disease. The shells would act like hypoder-

mic needles, pumping a deadly substance into the monster's system. Brian felt a shiver go up his spine. *Disease released in a populated area!* he thought. *This is crazy.*

A second general, a short, stocky man with a shaven head, proposed another type of tank shell. This one would be filled with cadmium—a substance that is often used to extinguish nuclear reactor fires.

That sounds promising, but will it work? Brian wondered. *Nick would know,* he concluded, missing his friend's knowledge of the sciences.

Suddenly, a wave of excitement rippled through the Diet chambers. Brian sat up and craned his neck. At the far end of the room, he saw a group of officials—some in military uniform—escorting Dr. Nobeyama to a table.

Brian gasped. The aged scientist looked even older and more frail than the last time Brian had seen him. *This crisis is killing him...*

Finally, the officer at the podium ended his speech. A third high-ranking military officer followed. He gave a brief statement about the defenses in and around Tokyo. He also stated that the special cadmium tank shells were ready. The officer concluded by saying that he hoped Dr. Nobeyama could suggest a poison that would kill Godzilla.

The scientist sat stony-faced, listening to the military briefings. Finally, Dr. Nobeyama rose. He was led to the center of the chamber by a soldier wearing a spit-and-polish uniform and white gloves. The room fell silent.

Dr. Nobeyama looked out at the audience and bowed slightly. Then, in a voice that was almost a whisper, he spoke to the rulers of Japan and, via satellite, to the people of the world.

"Ladies and gentlemen," he began. "I have presented my final report on the monster Godzilla to the Japanese government and the military leaders. This report, I am sad to say, is being ignored. For *that* reason, I now must present my findings to the world, in the hope that sanity will prevail."

He paused dramatically and shuffled the papers in his hand.

"In my opinion, a military attack on Godzilla would be a waste of time. It will only result in senseless loss of life and more destruction of property.

"All the evidence I have unearthed about Godzilla points to only one conclusion. The monster is immune to bombs, bullets, missiles, and rockets. Godzilla is, for all intents and purposes, indestructible!"

Angry shouts greeted Dr. Nobeyama's startling words. Then the whole Diet erupted in chaos. At the center of it all, the old man stood his ground defiantly.

Dr. Nobeyama continued his speech, though many of the voices tried to shout him down.

"Godzilla is not a natural being," he said. "The creature is not a product of evolution or natural selection. Godzilla was born in the radioactive fire of the hydrogen bomb—he has mutated beyond anything we understand.

"Bombs will confuse Godzilla, missiles will

make him angry. But no weapon, except perhaps a direct attack using a nuclear bomb, can possibly harm him. Because nuclear bombs cannot be used near population centers, we must stop this useless attack on Godzilla before it begins."

More shouts and angry denunciations were heard. The chairman pounded his gavel and demanded order.

"I have presented my report, and other scientists agree with my conclusions. Attack Godzilla if you must, but be aware that the creature cannot be killed by conventional weapons!"

With that, Dr. Nobeyama gathered up his papers and slowly made his way out of the crowded Diet chambers. Angry shouts followed him.

Brian wanted to rush to Dr. Nobeyama's side, but he knew that the old man would be busy briefing other scientists. So he stayed, and listened to speech after speech, for the next three hours.

Finally, it was decided that the Japanese Self-Defense Force would launch an attack on Godzilla that very evening, using the cadmium shells. Troops were mobilized. Equipment was moving into position. Everything was on schedule.

At dusk, the army would attack.

But will these cadmium shells really work? Brian wondered again.

"Cadmium shells will *never* work," Nick Gordon declared. "Cadmium is fine if you want to put out a nuclear fire. But it won't stop a nuclear chain reaction—which is what Godzilla *is!*"

"What makes you so certain Dr. Nobeyama is

correct?" Lieutenant Takado asked. "Many scientists don't agree with him."

"But *you* saw the film," Nick argued. "Wonder Lizard heals instantly. He *can't* be killed."

"But Dr. Nobeyama's work is still theoretical," the lieutenant argued. "Science still has limitations—"

"Science has nothing to *do* with it," Nick interrupted passionately. "This attack is all about politics, not science."

"Hai!" Yoshi said in agreement. "Even when politicians don't know what to do, they must do *something* to justify their existence."

The three of them sat in Lieutenant Takado's tent, which was lit by a single kerosene lantern. The tent was set up only a mile away from the flat plain where, at dawn, tanks would confront Godzilla.

Even as they spoke, the special cadmium shells were being delivered to tank commanders in the field.

All around them, Nick, Yoshi, and Lieutenant Takado could hear the sounds of the upcoming battle. Tanks and artillery rumbled toward the first line of defense, where bulldozers were carving defensive positions. Fuel and supply trucks filled with the specially designed ammunition followed the heavy armor to the front.

Overhead, Pave Low helicopters, equipped with special night-vision devices, circled the dark skies. Their job was to watch for Godzilla's approach and warn the army if the creature changed direction.

Periodically, the tent's radio crackled with situation updates and the latest reports on Godzilla's movements. There was excitement, and apprehension, in the air. Every nerve was on edge. No one knew what the morning would bring. The question was debated all over the camp, and in every tank, truck, and aircraft.

Would the new cadmium shells stop Godzilla?

Finally, after listening to another update from the choppers, Nick rose and stretched. "I'm going to hit the sleeping bag," he announced.

"Yes," Lieutenant Takado said. "We should all get some sleep. Tomorrow will be a momentous day."

Hundreds of miles away, in Tokyo, Brian sat with his uncle, Admiral Willis, and a dejected Dr. Nobeyama. The mood was grim. Dr. Nobeyama was convinced that the cadmium shells would fail. The admiral tended to agree with him.

Worse still, Dr. Nobeyama was certain that the cadmium would force Godzilla to find and consume a nuclear reactor core to replenish his strength. The resulting release of nuclear radiation might become an even bigger threat than Godzilla himself.

"But if the cadmium shells won't work," Brian asked, "then what can we do? Is humanity helpless?"

Dr. Nobeyama and Admiral Willis exchanged glances. Then Dr. Nobeyama spoke. "There is a glimmer of hope," he replied.

"You've found a weakness?" Brian asked excitedly.

"Perhaps," the Japanese scientist said noncommittally. "But it is only a theory..."

"Please explain it to me," Brian pleaded. The old man paused, his face unreadable. Then, finally, he nodded.

"There is a theory that dinosaurs did not become extinct millions of years ago. Some paleontologists believe the dinosaurs evolved because of climactic changes."

"The theory is that some species of dinosaurs evolved into modern birds," Brian interjected. "Isn't that correct?"

"Yes," Dr. Nobeyama answered. "You are correct."

"But how can an obscure theory on dinosaur evolution help us now?" Brian pressed.

"Through the equipment on the harpoon you fired, we learned much about Godzilla's physical nature," the scientist said. "We managed to get an EEG. That is a reading of Godzilla's brain waves. We learned that Godzilla's brain is very similar to a modern bird's brain—though vastly larger, of course."

"You see, son," Admiral Willis spoke up. "Dr. Nobeyama believes that Godzilla may respond to the same sounds that a bird responds to. And that's good news for us!"

"How?" Brian said, feeling hopeful for the first time since he had come face-to-face with the monster called Godzilla.

"Do you remember all that trouble last year—about the bird sanctuary near the U.S. Naval Base in Okinawa?"

Brian recalled some of the controversy. "Rare species of birds were at risk of being killed by American aircraft as they took off and landed," he said.

"Do you know how the problem was solved?" the admiral asked. Brian shook his head.

"A group at the Pentagon designed a bird alarm system—a high-frequency sound that only the birds could hear. Whenever planes took off, the guys in the tower turned on the alarm—"

"And it scared all the birds away!" Brian said, thinking fast.

"Exactly!" said the admiral, grinning.

Brian turned to Dr. Nobeyama. "So you think we can design an alarm that would frighten Godzilla away?"

"Not exactly," the doctor replied. "But I think we *can* devise a type of high-frequency sound *lure*—"

"Yes," the admiral interrupted. "Right now, I have some U.S. Navy sound technicians working on the problem. They say that, with Godzilla's brain-wave recordings, they are pretty sure they can come up with a lure of some kind. Perhaps in the next few days—"

"Yes," Dr. Nobeyama said earnestly. "They *must* come up with a workable lure before Godzilla arrives in Tokyo!"

"*Is* he coming to Tokyo?" Brian asked.

"I am certain of it," Dr. Nobeyama said ominously. "He came here once before, in 1954. Godzilla is *drawn* here...for some reason we do not fully understand."

"Why?" Brian asked.

The doctor scratched his head. "I can only speculate," he said. "Perhaps this area was once the creature's spawning grounds—or feeding grounds.

"Perhaps Godzilla is a territorial creature, and he thinks that Tokyo is *his* territory. Whatever the reason, I am sure that Godzilla is coming here—and very soon."

CHAPTER 16

ARMORED ATTACK!

June 8, 1998, 5:57 A.M.
Third Armored Battalion
Northeast of Onomichi, on the San-yo plain

Lieutenant Takado lifted the heavy steel hatch of the armored fighting vehicle and hopped out. She was followed almost immediately by Yoshi and Nick, who were both glad to be out in the open air again. They'd spent the better part of an hour bumping around inside the cramped quarters of the armored vehicle. It had been a rough ride.

"Don't these things have shock absorbers?" Nick whined, rubbing his bottom.

They stepped aside as the armored fighting vehicle gunned its diesel engine, turned completely around, and drove back the way it had come. Dirt and chunks of earth splattered Nick's J. Crew safari pants. He jumped backward.

The vehicle's steel treads dug up the earth, leaving a trail of deep grooves. They watched as it rolled out of sight over a barren hill. Soon, even the sound of its squeaky treads died, and they were alone on the quiet plain.

"We walk from here," Lieutenant Takado informed them. "The front lines are not very far, and we have our own observation post."

Yoshi and Nick lifted their gear and followed. The Japanese youth struggled under the weight of both his video camera and his backpack, which contained a portable satellite link. This equipment would enable him to send his taped images to INN headquarters.

Nick carried a bag containing blank videotapes, as well as his own portable tape recorder and plenty of audiocassettes.

During the *Kongo-Maru* attack, Nick had discovered how useful just speaking his thoughts into a recorder really was. He had been able to give a verbal eyewitness account of the action, without missing a thing. *I could never have recalled it all without my tapes,* Nick reminded himself.

He remembered how Brian had teased him for using the exact same method that reporter Stephen Martin had used forty-odd years before. Martin's book, *This Is Tokyo,* was mostly transcribed from his own voice tapes, made during Godzilla's rampage.

"I thought you said that Stephen Martin's techniques were old-fashioned," Brian had said when he saw Nick's machine.

"I said his *reporting* was old-fashioned," Nick replied defensively. "As far as using a tape recorder is concerned—hey, it works."

The day before, Nick had been surprised to see what the tank treads had done to the otherwise superb Japanese highway system. The roads leading up to the battleground had become pitted with giant potholes from the treads of millions of tons of armored vehicles.

Now Nick was shocked to see the damage that these same military vehicles had done to the landscape. Fields of grass and small copses of trees had been flattened. Tracks were everywhere, digging deep furrows into the rich earth.

Godzilla hasn't arrived yet, but the destruction has already begun, Nick thought grimly. He spoke those words into his tape recorder as they hiked to the observation post.

Ahead of them, the horizon was filled with dirty black smoke. There were occasional flashes, followed by the sound of the explosions rolling over them a moment later. Each flash illuminated the gigantic figure of Godzilla.

Again, Nick was awed in the monster's presence. *There's no way I can describe this*, he thought, frustrated by his limited narrative powers. *I guess you just have to be here*.

But he knew that he had to try. *It's my job*, he reminded himself every time he felt like giving up.

Stumbling over the tortured earth, Lieutenant Takado led them on a half-hour hike. Finally, she pointed to an industrial site surrounded by a chain-link fence. "Our post is over there," she told them.

When they reached the fence's padlocked gate, Lieutenant Takado reached into her pack and produced a key.

Once through the gate, she pointed to a factory tower of some kind. It was a steel frame covered with thick pipes. More pipes ran up through the middle of the tower. A huge tank was at the top.

She led them to the base of the tower, stopping at a doorway that led to a metal cage. Nick looked up. At the top of the hundred-and-fifty-foot tower, he saw a small hut with observation windows. The hut was constructed of corrugated metal sheets.

"Get in," Lieutenant Takado said, opening the door to the metal cage. Nick and Yoshi stepped into the primitive elevator. The lieutenant pressed the button and, with a jolt, the shaky elevator began to rise.

As the creaky cage neared the top, Nick and Yoshi admired the view. "You certainly know your way around," Nick remarked.

Lieutenant Takado smiled. "I scouted this place myself," she informed him.

Soon, they reached a high catwalk. The elevator jerked to a halt and the steel doors slid open. They followed a narrow walkway until they reached another door. This one was unlocked, and they entered the tiny metal hut.

Inside was a cheap wooden desk, a bare overhead light, and two battered chairs.

"The accommodations aren't much," Nick quipped. "But the view *is* spectacular."

The factory was on top of a low hill, and Nick could see that they occupied the highest ground for miles around.

Looking out the windows, which lacked glass or even a screen, they could see the battle lines spread out before them. The Japanese tanks were lined up in three rows, waiting for Godzilla's arrival. Over their heads, the skies were alive with military helicopters. Yoshi tapped Nick's shoulder and pointed.

Nick saw it, too—an ABC helicopter with a huge camera mounted on its fuselage. Nick scanned the morning sky and saw three more news choppers— one from NHK, the Japanese network; one from the Cable News Network; and another from the British Broadcasting Corporation.

Finally, Yoshi spotted the chopper from INN and showed his partner.

"Max Hulse is up there," Nick remarked. "They should play his reports over a loudspeaker—they might actually put Godzilla to *sleep!*"

As they watched, the news helicopters moved slowly toward the front lines. Each helicopter focused its powerful cameras at the horizon. Looming there was the creature called Godzilla, silhouetted by the explosions and fires in his wake.

Nick's heart raced in anticipation. He felt strangely alive in the middle of this battlefield. He turned to Yoshi. His face was lit with excitement, too. *No wonder Yoshi wants to become a war correspondent,* Nick mused. *There is something powerful and alive about a battlefield. It's so... intense!*

Quickly, Yoshi set up his camera and assembled the portable satellite link. There was plenty of electricity supplied to the tower, courtesy of a nuclear power plant somewhere behind them—and in Godzilla's path.

While Yoshi spoke to technicians back at INN headquarters, Lieutenant Takado opened a plastic envelope containing a military MRE—Meal, Ready to Eat. She offered one to Nick, who politely declined.

Suddenly, as one, the front line of tanks began to rev up their idling engines. The tanks, Japanese-made Type 74s and 75s, had round turrets and long 105-millimeter cannons. They looked very different from the U.S. front-line battle tank, the M1A1 Abrams, which had a square, boxlike turret.

Lieutenant Takado's military radio squawked. A stern voice began giving orders in Japanese. Nick looked at her. "What's going on?" he asked.

"The general has just given the order," she answered. "The attack is about to begin."

As the engines continued to rev up, tank commanders popped their heads out of the hatches on top of their turrets. They scanned the horizon with binoculars.

In a matter of minutes, all guns were pointed at Godzilla.

Then, again as one, the tanks in the first line moved forward. They approached the monster slowly over the rough terrain. From the vantage point of the tower, the armored tanks looked like turtles as they crawled toward Godzilla.

Undaunted by the line of tanks that moved to block his way, the monster approached.

Now the thunder of Godzilla's footsteps could be heard over the noise of the tanks. Finally, the monster noticed the tiny pests that had come to hurt him.

Puzzled at the intruders, Godzilla turned his head to one side in curiosity. He seemed to wonder just what these things were.

Suddenly, a yellow trail of fire shot across the

slate gray morning sky. The signal flare burst into green incandescence right in front of the creature's nose. Godzilla reared back and opened his huge maw.

A terrible, echoing roar of confusion issued from the creature's throat.

And at that moment, fire and smoke and steel belched out of a hundred cannons. The first line of tanks fired in unison. The thunderous sound rolled across the San-yo plain. Burning shells sped toward the creature with a whistling howl.

Nick covered his ears. The tower vibrated from the ear-shattering din. For a moment, Godzilla seemed to be engulfed in smoke and flames. Hundreds of shells burst against his hide and penetrated his flesh. His roar of pain and rage rolled across the plain. Godzilla's mighty cry drowned out the sound of the tanks.

Nick felt a stab of fear. Yoshi, too, was shaken. But the young Japanese stubbornly continued to film footage of the attack.

Another volley of tank shells, fired from the second row of tanks, slammed against Godzilla within moments of the first. More explosions flashed all over the creature's chest, neck, and face. A third volley followed. Then a fourth.

The whole world seemed to shake. Nick turned off his tape recorder—the sound level meter was reacting wildly to the terrible roar of battle. The machine was useless in this chaos.

Smoke billowed across the battlefield, obscuring Godzilla like a shroud. Nick's eyes strained to pierce the haze, which seemed to roll toward them on the breeze. Occasionally he could catch a glimpse of the monster through the cauldron of smoke and fire.

For a moment, Godzilla's eyes seemed to stare back at Nick through the haze.

Then the guns were quieted. The smoke cleared.

To Nick's surprise, a terrible roar filled his ears. *I can't believe it.*

Godzilla was still standing! Despite the highly praised cadmium shells, the creature seemed totally unaffected by the munitions that had been fired into his body at almost point-blank range. Even Yoshi gasped in surprise. Lieutenant Takado frowned, then keyed her radio.

The tanks in the front line began to back up or veer away. The entire line was soon scattered as the tanks—now out of ammunition—tried to flee from the battlefield. But Godzilla directed his reptilian gaze down at a dozen vehicles on his right. His dorsal fins glimmered, and with an angry grunt, he spat blue fire.

As the lights illuminated his bony spines, Godzilla rained radioactive death down on the tanks at its feet. Nick watched in choking horror as the heat began to melt the vehicles.

The tanks glowed redly. The cannons went first—they slowly began to dip toward the ground as they turned to molten metal. Several of the tanks blew up almost immediately, their turrets flying into the air. Other tanks soon followed.

In less than a minute, thirteen tanks had been reduced to melted steel. Their four-man crews had been incinerated where they sat. There had been no hope of escape.

The attack was broken. The second and third

lines of tanks backed up, turned around, and fled. They fired their cannons at Godzilla to cover their retreat, but the fire was undirected and ineffective. Godzilla stepped forward among the fleeing vehicles.

Again and again, Godzilla's feet came down on the retreating tanks. The monster crushed men and machinery where they stood, grinding them into piles of mangled metal.

The battle was almost over before it began. It was a rout for Godzilla.

While Nick, Yoshi, and Lieutenant Takado watched helplessly, the best men and machinery of the Japanese Self-Defense Force were smashed by Godzilla's onslaught.

Nick turned to Lieutenant Takado. She was near tears. *She probably knows some of the soldiers down there,* Nick realized. Just then, the lieutenant's radio crackled to life. She swallowed hard, regained her composure, and replied.

A long conversation in Japanese followed. When she finally signed off, she turned to the two reporters.

"We must go," she stated. "The attack is over, and as soon as the tanks are out of the area, the army is going to launch a long-distance rocket attack. We will be in danger if we stay."

Nick and Yoshi exchanged glances. They saw the same determination in each other's eyes.

"We're staying," the two men said in unison.

Lieutenant Takado looked at them. "You will be killed," she stated simply. "Nothing can be gained by sacrificing yourselves for a *news story*."

"But we have a job to do," Nick insisted.

"Look up," she said, pointing. Nick and Yoshi turned their eyes toward the gray morning sky. The news helicopters were flying over their heads, away from the battle.

"They have been ordered to leave, too," Lieutenant Takado said. "Soon this area will be a killing field, and hundreds of high-explosive fragmentation rockets will rain down from the sky."

Again, Yoshi and Nick exchanged glances. They nodded.

"Okay." Nick surrendered with a mock salute. "Where to, Lieutenant?"

"On the other side of the factory, a rented off-road vehicle awaits us," she told the two.

"Rented!" Nick said in surprise.

Lieutenant Takado nodded. "I rented it myself. I did not want to trust the military to get us out of here if…things fell apart."

"You're quite a gal, Emiko!" Nick said, his admiration real.

She accepted the compliment with a nod. "We have fifteen minutes to get as far away from here as possible."

CHAPTER 17

"LAUNCH THE ROCKETS!"

June 8, 1998, 8:01 A.M.
Japanese field command post
Somewhere on the San-yo plain

"The tanks have been driven back, commander," the officer informed General Shuji Kamata grimly. "The forward wave of the attack has sustained heavy losses. Much of the First Battalion has been disabled or destroyed."

The general's eyes narrowed. *So many men gone*, he thought sadly, *and no time to honor them now*. The general remembered that his first duty was to protect the living.

The general spoke. "Warn the field commanders that a rocket attack will begin in fifteen minutes."

Captain Honda, his second-in-command, saluted, then ran off to carry out the commander's orders.

Glancing at the map spread out in front of him, General Kamata considered his options. *At least I can cover the First Battalion's retreat*, he told himself. *But if the rockets don't halt Gojira's advance, then there is nothing that will stop him from reaching the nuclear power plant in the next twenty-four hours.*

General Kamata rubbed his tired eyes and planned his retreat.

Fifty yards from the command center, a line of unusual trucks waited under camouflage netting. The vehicles resembled ordinary trucks with green canvas tents mounted on the back, but these tents hid a deadly cargo.

At Captain Honda's command, soldiers pulled away the canvas covering from each truck, revealing two lethal-looking rockets mounted on rail launchers. The rockets, called Type 68s, had two-hundred-pound high-explosive warheads.

Engines began coughing to life, and the air was filled with the smell of diesel fuel. The launchers slowly tilted upward, pointing their rockets at the overcast sky. There were twenty-five trucks, carrying a total of fifty Type 68 rockets, which were now being aimed at Godzilla.

The monster was thirteen miles away.

As the minutes ticked away, the rockets were readied for firing.

Two miles south of the industrial tower where Lieutenant Takado, Nick, and Yoshi were packing up their gear and preparing to flee, three tanks of the First Battalion were racing through the countryside.

They were in full retreat.

Having been fortunate enough to escape Godzilla's attack, the Type 75 tanks sped over the rugged terrain as fast as they could go—about twenty-five miles per hour.

The turret hatch on the lead tank popped open,

and Sergeant Tsuburaya, the tank commander, stuck his head out warily. He looked behind him.

Damn! he thought. He could still see Godzilla. The monster's head towered above a line of factory buildings. Sergeant Tsuburaya wasn't sure what the range of Godzilla's fire was—and he didn't want to find out.

"Drive faster!" he barked to the driver.

The man looked up at his commander. His face was dripping with sweat—the tank's air conditioner had failed hours before. He fought the controls. "I could only drive faster over a paved highway!" the driver declared with more than a touch of insubordination.

Sergeant Tsuburaya sneered at the man. "Then I'll find you one!" he cried. Sitting up in the hatch, the sergeant scanned the horizon. *There!* he said to himself.

Behind a wall of trees and bushes, Sergeant Tsuburaya spotted a ribbon of roadway. "Turn right!" he screamed to his driver. Then he repeated the command to the other tank commanders. The three Type 75 tanks swung right. But when they neared the highway, they could find no opening in the tree line through which to drive.

"Crash through!" Sergeant Tsuburaya commanded the driver. The treads skidded in the dirt as the fifty-ton tank slammed into the tree line.

Suddenly, there was a flash of blue fire and a shower of sparks. Sergeant Tsuburaya ducked down into the tank as burning hot sparks rained down through the hatch and onto the crew.

"What happened?" the gunner asked the

sergeant as he brushed ashes off his uniform. Sergeant Tsuburaya shook his head.

"I'm not sure," he said breathlessly. "I think we hit a telephone pole or something."

Sergeant Tsuburaya's guess was close. His tank had actually hit an electrical transformer—a vital part of the power grid in the area. The collision had done minimal damage to the tank, which now sped down the highway with two others following behind. But much damage had been done to the transformer.

In less than a second, the power had been knocked out in a ten-mile radius—a radius that included the factory tower.

Just as Nick, Yoshi, and Lieutenant Takado were about to leave the tiny hut, the bare overhead bulb suddenly went out. Nick looked up at it.

"The power must have gone out," he remarked casually. Then he paled and looked at Lieutenant Takado. She had a horrified expression on her face.

Yoshi looked up. He sensed something was wrong. Then it dawned on him, too. The elevator wouldn't work without electric power.

"Are we trapped up here?" Nick immediately asked.

Lieutenant Takado shook her head uncertainly. "There is a ladder," she said. "But I don't think it is very good...or very easy to get to."

"Let's go see!" Nick said, rushing out the door and onto the catwalk.

A minute later, they were staring at the ladder. It

seemed to reach all the way to the bottom of the tower, all right. But the problem was that the ladder was on the other end of a missing catwalk. The railing for the catwalk was there, but there was no platform.

"This sucks," said Nick. "What do we do now?"

Yoshi dropped his gear and examined the problem. His eyes traced the maze of girders, pipes, and cables.

"Look," he said after a moment. "I think we can climb up to that pipe there, swing over that girder there, then follow that thin pipe on the left...it leads right up to the ladder."

Nick and Lieutenant Takado listened again as he repeated his instructions.

"I can do it," the woman said at last.

Nick swallowed hard. *I hate heights,* he moaned. Then he nodded. "Yeah, I can do it, too." He looked down at his wristwatch. "But we'd better abandon anything we can't carry and get started right now. We've only got eleven minutes!"

The five-man crews of each of the rocket launchers were completing their final preparations. There was less than three minutes remaining before launch time.

Captain Honda circled the camp, making final preparations, too. As the moments ticked by, he readied the radio for final orders. With less than a minute left, he returned to the command center and approached General Kamata.

"All is in readiness," he informed the general.

"And the area—is it clear?" the general asked.

"The order to evacuate has been given to all field commanders, sir," he answered. "They have had fifteen minutes—and we are running out of time. Godzilla is closing in."

"Has the observation aircraft reported in?" General Kamata asked.

"Hai," Captain Honda said. "He reports no tanks or armored personnel carriers in the area."

The general paused. Then he nodded his head grimly.

"Launch the rockets!" he commanded.

The order was forwarded to the vehicle commanders instantly. Within seconds, the roar of rocket engines filled the area as the first Type 68 solid-fuel rockets left their rail launchers and climbed into the gray skies.

Despite their fancy footwork, it had taken Nick, Yoshi, and Lieutenant Takado five minutes to reach the ladder, and another two minutes to climb to the bottom. Yoshi had reluctantly left behind his satellite link and the bigger of his two cameras. He had kept the small camera and all of his videocassettes strapped on his back as he made the precarious climb down the tower.

Nick, too, had managed to keep his tape recorder and tapes.

When they were all on the ground again, Nick checked his watch. "The rocket attack is supposed to take place in less than four minutes," he said ominously.

"Let's go," Lieutenant Takado replied, taking off at a run. The three of them crossed the factory floor, running past huge machines and a maze of pipes and tubes, bins and vats. Once, as they ran past a window, Nick pointed.

Godzilla was very close to the factory. They could hear the sound of explosions and the collapse of buildings in the monster's wake. Yoshi and Nick exchanged glances.

They reached a huge doorway made of corrugated steel. Lieutenant Takado swung the door open.

"The rental car is on the other side of that building," she said, pointing to another factory structure fifty yards across a paved, open area that looked like a parking lot.

"Let's go—" Nick cried, but was interrupted when Lieutenant Takado grabbed his arm.

"Listen!" she hissed.

Nick and Yoshi paused. Then they heard it. A high-pitched whistling sound. It was getting louder—and closer.

"The rocket attack has begun!" Lieutenant Takado cried. "Get down on the ground! Over there!" She pointed to a huge piece of heavy machinery. The three of them dived under the metal structure just as the first rocket struck the earth outside.

"Cover your heads!" Lieutenant Takado cried as a terrible explosion rocked the entire factory complex. Another explosion quickly followed, showering dust down on the cowering trio.

Boom! Boom! BOOM! BOOM! BAMMMMMM!

Blast after blast shook the building. One rocket struck the opposite end of the complex, blowing the roof right off it. After the blast, Nick could see the tower they once occupied through the hole in the roof. It was burning.

Then another rocket struck the factory. More dirt and debris rained down on them. The burning tower twisted, then slowly fell like a giant tree chopped down by a lumberjack. In the noise of the rocket attack, Nick couldn't hear the sound of the tower striking the earth.

Outside, Godzilla howled as rockets rained down on him. Explosions tore up the earth all around the creature. Some of the rockets struck Godzilla directly, bringing more roars of rage.

Godzilla was knocked off his mighty feet by the power of high-explosive shells that kept on coming, and coming, and coming.

In the skies above the terrible killing field, the two-man crew of a small military scout aircraft observed the destruction. As the plane circled the sky, the pilot and co-pilot tried to see through the billowing smoke and blazing fires.

"Godzilla is down!" the man in the observer's position said. The pilot strained his eyes, but all he could see was the mighty beast's flashing tail. Suddenly, a blue-white jet of radioactive fire shot up into the sky from the chaos below them. The blast was undirected, but it startled the two men.

"There is a factory down there," the observer noted after he regained his composure. "Some of the rockets are hitting it."

"It's a good thing there's no one inside," the pilot remarked.

*   *   *

After an eternity of explosions, of choking smoke, of dust and dirt, the attack subsided.

Warily, Nick opened his eyes and raised his head. Smoke billowed through the factory, which was mostly shattered now. He saw Yoshi, who was bending over Lieutenant Takado. She was not moving.

Nick jumped up and crawled to her side. He looked at her.

"Is she okay?" he asked urgently.

Yoshi nodded. "She was hit on the head by debris," he told Nick. "I have stopped the bleeding."

Nick and Yoshi heard the woman moan. Then she opened her eyes and stared up at them.

"Welcome back, Emiko," Yoshi said in Japanese.

She smiled up at him. "The attack is over?" she asked.

"Hai!" Yoshi replied.

She sat up immediately. "Then we have to go," she said. "If Godzilla has not been stopped, this attack will be followed by others."

At that moment, Godzilla's distinctive roar echoed across the San-yo plain. All three of them shivered.

"Come on," Nick said. He and Yoshi helped Emiko scramble to her feet. They warily stepped out into the gray morning—made even gloomier by the smoke and dust that still lingered in the air after the rocket attack.

Again, Lieutenant Takado pointed to the building on the other side of the parking lot. The building had sustained some minor damage, but remained mostly intact. "The car is over there."

Together, the trio ran across the pavement and circled the building. When they got to the other side, Nick halted in his tracks. Emiko and Yoshi stopped too.

A red rental car, its finish still shiny, sat next to the battered building. Unfortunately, much of the damaged structure had collapsed—and was lying on top of the car.

Behind the mostly intact engine and front seat, the rental car had been totally crushed by tons of steel.

Nick stared at the unwelcome sight. "I don't think you'll get your deposit back."

At that moment, they heard a high-pitched whistling that sounded ominously familiar.

"The second wave of the rocket attack has begun," said the lieutenant.

Nick looked at Yoshi. "Not again!"

"Come on," cried Emiko. "We must seek shelter!"

CHAPTER 18

THE BATTLE ON
THE BRIDGE

June 11, 1998, 9:16 A.M.
INN newsroom
Tokyo, Japan

Brian stepped into the crowded newsroom. He took a look at the television monitors, then he looked around the room. He spotted Mr. Takao's grizzled features. The newsroom chief was approaching Blackthorn Adams's office. Brian quickly cornered the older Japanese man.

"Any word?" Brian asked eagerly.

The man frowned. "Still nothing."

"Brian! Over here!" May McGovern cried from the elevators, her auburn ponytail bouncing as she rushed toward him. "Mr. Endicott wants to see you immediately."

Brian followed her back to the elevators, and May held the door open. When the elevator began to rise, she turned to Brian. Her expression was hopeful. But Brian shook his head sadly.

"Sorry, May. Still no word from any of them," he

informed her. May's expression quickly turned grave.

"Don't worry," Brian added, trying to cheer her up. "If anybody can take care of himself, it's Nick. And with Lieutenant Takado and Yoshi with him, he'll be fine."

"Then why haven't we heard from them?" she asked, a catch in her voice.

"Since the rocket attack three days ago, that whole section of Honshu is in total chaos," he said. "The highways are choked with refugees, and only military vehicles are permitted into the area. There's no communications in or out, no flyovers are permitted, and no live news reports either." Brian paused.

"Look, May, I was going over the reports this morning. The military can't evacuate people fast enough. The wounded are still out in the fields, and emergency procedures have completely broken down.

"It makes sense that Nick and Yoshi are just stuck out there somewhere in the middle of that mess," he said as the elevator doors slid open on the executive floor.

"I'm sure that they're just fine." Brian tried to sound more confident than he really felt. But by the expression of torment on May's pretty face, he could see he'd failed miserably.

The fact was, Brian hadn't told May everything. There were unconfirmed reports of looting, and even murder, coming out of the emergency areas. One story going around was about a bunch of *yakuza* gangsters—the Japanese version of the Mafia—who had hijacked a military helicopter, killed the soldiers, and used the chopper to safely carry out the booty they'd looted from abandoned towns.

Could his friends survive in such chaos? Brian wondered. He prayed they could.

"Come in, Mr. Shimura," Everett Endicott said as May ushered Brian into the bureau chief's office.

Brian sat down, and the two men faced each other. Endicott had bags under his eyes. He looked tired. But then, everybody did. The portly man rubbed his bloodshot eyes and cleared his throat.

"Have you heard from your uncle lately—in the last few days, perhaps?"

"No, I haven't," Brian replied honestly. "I thought the admiral was working with Dr. Nobeyama and the Japanese Self-Defense Force."

"He's missing," Endicott said. "And so is Dr. Nobeyama."

Brian sat up straight. "Missing?" he cried.

Endicott nodded. "For at least forty-eight hours now…since Dr. Nobeyama presented the military leaders with his proposal to lure Godzilla away from Japan."

Brian shook his head in disgust. "A proposal that was flatly rejected," he said bitterly, "in favor of a pointless rocket attack that did more damage to the area than Godzilla himself!"

"Well," the bureau chief replied. "That's not our concern—we only *report* the news. Which is why I sent for you. Since Gordon and Masahara are...out of touch, I'm sending you out into the field again. In less than an hour, you'll join Max Hulse and Blackthorn Adams on the INN helipad."

"Just where am I going this time?" Brian asked, excited about getting field work again—but at the same time not happy about being sent away from headquarters while Nick and Yoshi were still missing.

"The Japanese Self-Defense Force will make one final assault to try to stop Godzilla from reaching Tokyo," Endicott said. "They are going to launch a combined air, sea, and ground assault at the Seto Ohashi Bridge. We've been given permission to broadcast the event."

Brian swallowed hard. "So Godzilla is still moving along the coast of the Inland Sea," he whispered.

"Yes," Endicott answered. "And there is bad news, too, which will be released to the public around noon."

Brian sat forward in his chair, all ears.

"Last night, Godzilla destroyed a nuclear power plant near Kurashiki," the bureau chief said evenly.

"Then—"

"Yes. Godzilla has absorbed the nuclear cores of two reactors. That means he's even stronger now. He's increased his speed, and is heading for the water again. The army is absolutely certain Godzilla will move through the Inland Sea and swim directly to Tokyo—*if* this final attack at the bridge fails."

Three hours later, Brian sat in the personnel com-

partment of a U.S. Marine Corps Blackhawk helicopter—on loan to the INN news service for use
during the crisis.

Along with Brian, a British cameraman named
Ian Smelt and science correspondent Blackthorn
Adams rode in the helicopter.

Another Marine Corps Blackhawk followed
behind. That one contained Nick's nemesis, Max
Hulse, and an INN technical crew. There was also a
small contingent of Marines on both Blackhawks.
Their job was to protect American lives, even if the
Americans in question were members of the hated
news media.

"Three minutes to touchdown," the sergeant, a
huge black man with sharp features and bulky
Kevlar body armor, informed the passengers. Brian
nodded and looked out the window. He saw the
blue-green waters of the Inland Sea twinkling in
the sunlight far below.

Suddenly, the Blackhawk banked and swung
over land. It began to descend rapidly. Brian's
stomach flew into his throat. He swallowed and
strained his eyes but could see no signs of the
chaos that ruled the island below.

The helicopter kicked up dust as it settled onto
the landing site, a parking lot outside a now-desert-
ed shopping mall near the abandoned city of
Tamano. The Marines jumped out of the chopper
and took defensive positions. Brian, Ian Smelt,
and Blackthorn Adams made a less dramatic departure.

On the other end of the parking lot, Brian
noticed an INN helicopter.

An INN technician, whom Brian recognized, waved them to the entranceway of the mall. Brian took off in a jog, running to the man's side.

"We've got a setup on the roof," the man said. "Cameras, satellite uplinks, telescopes—the whole shebang."

While they spoke, the second Blackhawk helicopter landed, and Max Hulse joined them.

A few minutes later, Blackthorn, Ian Smelt, Max Hulse, and Brian all crowded into a small service elevator and rode it to the top. When the doors slid open, Brian was surprised to see that they were already on the roof. Another INN technician ran up to them.

"The attack is going to start in thirty minutes," he cried. "Godzilla is already visible through binoculars!"

But instead of trying to spot Godzilla, Brian examined the huge structure that spanned the Inland Sea. He was amazed at the size of the Seto Ohashi Bridge. It seemed to go on forever.

"Some bridge, eh?" Ian Smelt said.

Brian nodded.

"That's the longest bridge in the world," the young British cameraman added with enthusiasm.

Blackthorn Adams, who was awaiting his turn in front of the camera, joined in the conversation. "It's really six bridges built into a single span, you know," the science correspondent informed them. "The bridges connect a bunch of small islands that dot the Inland Sea, and join the main island of Honshu with the island of Shikoku. There's a highway and a rail line that use that bridge daily.

"The builders claim that the cables used in the construction are long enough to wrap around the Earth several times. They also claim that the bridge is earthquake-proof."

"I think we're about to see if the bridge is *Godzilla*-proof," Ian Smelt interrupted, pointing toward the span. "Here he comes!"

The morale was low among the forces stationed on the Seto Ohashi Bridge. Many of the men felt that they were going to be sacrificed for no good reason. The soldiers had all heard about the futile attack on the San-yo plain. Word was traveling through the ranks that guns, tanks, and bombs were like toys against Godzilla.

Rumor had it that Godzilla was virtually indestructible.

Even an emotional pep talk by General Nakamura failed to inspire the men. But despite their reservations, the men performed their duties obediently. As Godzilla approached, they lined the bridge with Type 75 tanks armed with the less-than-successful cadmium shells, as well as more multiple rocket launchers and a variety of towed and self-propelled artillery pieces.

The Seto Ohashi Bridge was bristling with guns. All were pointed at the approaching monster.

The sky, too, was filled with aircraft from the Japanese Air Force—F-15J Eagles purchased from the United States, mostly. They were armed with guided bombs, machine guns, and air-to-ground missiles.

On the water, two *Chikugo*-class frigates—the

Noshiro and the *Mogami*—followed Godzilla's every movement. The frigates were small, but they were the only warships that could navigate the shallow waters of the Inland Sea. They also sported fearsome, boxlike multiple rocket launchers on their decks, instead of the standard gun turrets most frigates are armed with.

Oblivious to the military might arrayed against him, Godzilla continued to wade through the sea, moving slowly toward the suspension bridge that blocked his path.

On the bridge, General Nakamura checked his watch, which was synchronized with the time-pieces on the ships below and in the aircraft above.

"Thirty seconds to attack!" he announced over the command radio.

A thousand men placed their sweat-slicked fingers on the triggers of cannons, machine guns, rocket launchers, and artillery pieces. Breathlessly, they awaited the general's final command.

"Ready...aim...*fire!*" General Nakamura cried over the radio.

Even from the vantage point on top of the shopping mall, miles away, Brian's ears were pounded by the tremendous sound of a thousand guns. The entire Seto Ohashi Bridge seemed to sway from the recoil of the tank and artillery cannons as they spat steel and fire at Godzilla.

The frigates, too, opened fire. Missiles streaked from the boxlike launchers, leaving trails of orange fire and white smoke in their wake.

Overhead, a dozen jets dived down out of the clouds and aimed their sights on Godzilla. The monster was soon engulfed in clouds of smoke and flame.

Godzilla bellowed in rage as the munitions struck him again and again. The beast covered his eyes with his mighty five-fingered claws. His gigantic tail thrashed, stirring up the waters of the Inland Sea. Powerful waves battered against the frigates with colossal force, but still the warships pressed on, pouring fire on the gigantic creature that loomed ahead.

The noise of the blasts and the echoing howls of the beast rolled across the sea and land. The clamor slammed against Brian's ears in waves, pounding his eardrums until he reached up and covered them with his hands. Still, the awesome sound penetrated his ears and made his chest vibrate. Brian closed his eyes, shutting out the terrible vision of destruction unfolding in front of him.

"Nothing can survive *that!*" Ian Smelt cried over the noise. "Godzilla's finished."

But Brian knew better. *Dr. Nobeyama is right. Nothing can kill Godzilla*, he said to himself. *The monster is like a force of nature, like a typhoon, an earthquake or a hurricane...*

Mankind is helpless against brute force such as this!

Unexpectedly, there was a split-second lull in the firing. It was just enough time for the Japanese fighters to dive down and drop their ordnance on Godzilla. But instead of explosives, Brian was surprised to see that the fighters were dropping guided bombs filled with napalm—burning jellied gasoline.

He watched in horror as Godzilla burst into flame!

In seconds, the greater part of Godzilla's body was covered with hot orange fire. The monster bellowed and flailed his arms wildly as the napalm scorched his head, neck, chest, and back.

Godzilla's wails of pain rolled across the water.

"God, how horrible," Ian Smelt muttered.

Then, as the F-15Js released the last of their bombs and climbed into the sky, a burst of blue fire streaked toward them. Two of the aircraft were engulfed in the radioactive stream and exploded instantly.

The other fighters kicked in their afterburners and flew away as fast as possible.

Still on fire, Godzilla dropped down, splashing into the Inland Sea. Waves washed over the frigate that was closest to the monster. The *Mogami* capsized as tons of water slammed against her.

Within moments, Godzilla rose again. Most of the chemical flames had now been extinguished. Yet parts of his arms, face, and head still smoldered, and he cried out in agony once more.

The tanks and artillery on the bridge resumed firing. But the barrage was much less intense. *They must be running low on ammunition,* Brian realized.

Whatever the reason for the weakened attack, it had tragic consequences. The diminished firepower allowed Godzilla to get alongside the Seto Ohashi Bridge.

As Godzilla loomed over the soldiers and tanks stationed on the bridge, the men began to abandon their posts. With nothing standing in his path but the span of the bridge itself, Godzilla charged.

The monster slammed his massive bulk against it. Incredibly, the structure held. Although the cables that reached from one end of the bridge to the other shook and vibrated, they did not break. But the men, tanks, trucks, and rocket launchers that dotted the span were not so fortunate.

As the bridge shook, everything on it was bounced violently around. Men and machines were tossed into the air. Helpless soldiers were thrown over the edge of the bridge. They plunged, screaming, into the waves that lapped against the foundation hundreds of feet below.

Godzilla flailed again. This time one of the towers cracked. When he slammed the bridge once more, several trucks exploded, spreading fire and burning fuel along the entire span. The screams of frightened men mingled with the sound of Godzilla's roar.

Again Godzilla struck, and, at last, the bridge gave way. It literally split into two, spilling vehicles and men into the Inland Sea.

In less than a minute, the entire span of the Seto Ohashi Bridge came tumbling down.

With a mighty roar of triumph, Godzilla moved past the tangled wreckage of steel cable, concrete, and vehicles. The frigate *Noshiro*'s path was blocked by the shattered bridge, but still the warship futilely fired missiles at Godzilla's retreating back.

As Brian watched from his vantage point on the shopping mall roof, Godzilla moved slowly away from the destruction. Smoke still poured off his body where the napalm had scorched him. But as Godzilla departed, he did not look back.

The battle at the bridge was over.

Sickened by the destruction he'd witnessed, Brian sank to the roof. He hung his head and blinked back tears. He sat, motionless and speechless, for a few moments. Then he felt a tap on his shoulder.

Ian stood over him. "We're going," he said. "Max is staying behind to wrap things up and give a final, on-camera report. But we've been ordered back to Tokyo."

Brian nodded dumbly and struggled to his feet. Without saying a word, he walked slowly toward the service elevator.

Forty-five minutes after the Blackhawks departed for Tokyo, Max Hulse and two technicians were loading the INN helicopter in preparation for their own departure.

Two Marines, including the stern-faced sergeant, served as their bodyguards. They were almost ready to lift off when three ragged figures appeared on the other end of the parking lot. The strangers began to shout and wave at the helicopter.

The figures began running toward the INN aircraft. The sergeant, wary of trouble, dropped to one knee in a defensive position. He pointed his M-16 at the strangers.

"Halt!" the Marine cried, raising his hand. Two of the figures slowed down, but the third kept coming. He was shouting something now, but the Marine couldn't hear him over the sound of the chopper's engine. Max Hulse turned and saw the man approaching.

"Halt and drop to the ground!" the Marine cried again, still pointing his weapon at the trio.

Now the youth in the lead slowed, but still approached warily. He continued to shout something. Finally, they understood what he was saying.

"Mr. Hulse!" the man shouted. The newsman heard his name being called. He reached down and touched the barrel of the sergeant's weapon.

"Let them come closer," the newsman said. Then he waved the three dirty figures forward. The tallest youth reached the helicopter first. He stopped when he saw the soldier, who still held the M-16 at the ready.

"Whoa," the man said. He wore a dirty safari jacket and tattered pants. He was covered in mud, as were the two who remained behind.

"I'm an American," he said. "Look!" He offered them his plastic I.D. card.

"I work for INN," the man insisted. Max Hulse took the plastic card out of the youth's grimy hand. The other two figures cautiously approached. The Marine was surprised to see that one of them was a woman.

"My name is Nick Gordon," the youth said. "And that's Yoshi Masahara and Lieutenant Emiko Takado. We've been following Godzilla for days—

since the rocket attack on the San-yo plain—and boy, do we have some great footage for *you!*"

Max Hulse smiled at the three of them. "Hop in," he said. "We'll take you back to Tokyo."

"Gee, thanks, Mr. Hulse," Nick said as he climbed into the chopper.

As he settled into his seat, Nick leaned over to Max Hulse.

"You know, Mr. Hulse," he said with a grin. "I'm a really big fan of yours…"

CHAPTER 19

TOKYO!

June 18, 1998, 10:27 A.M.
INN network headquarters
Tokyo, Japan

Brian sat in his cubicle, watching the monitor in front of him, which was tuned to CNN. The world was still on emergency footing, but things had been a bit calmer in the last few days.

After the terrible attack at the Seto Ohashi Bridge, Godzilla had moved through the Inland Sea virtually unopposed. When he hit the deep waters of the Pacific Ocean, he vanished from sight. Even the submarines that were detailed to follow the creature soon lost track of him in the silent depths of the ocean.

For over a week now, the people of Tokyo had lived in fear—waiting for the attack that they were sure would come.

After the debacle on the San-yo plain, the Japanese government was reluctant to order a city-wide evacuation of the capital. There was nowhere they could send the millions of people who lived in the Tokyo metropolitan area, anyway. All of the rail lines and highways southwest of the capital were smashed already. Many of the cities were leveled as well.

Despite the reluctance of the government to move people out of Tokyo, many citizens left on their own. The NHK network estimated that fully one-third of Tokyo's population had already fled. More were trying to leave. Airports and docks were jammed. Prices for airline tickets at first doubled, then tripled. Now you couldn't get a ticket out, at least not legitimately—they were available only on the black market, for exorbitant prices.

Godzilla's present location was still unknown. The one bright light in all the darkness was Nick and Yoshi's triumphant return to INN headquarters. In his heart of hearts, Brian had nearly given up hope of ever seeing his friends again. But they had defied the odds and happily returned from the dead.

The two men were given a heroes' welcome. News executives—including the ever-skeptical Everett P. Endicott—were thoroughly impressed with the massive amount of footage and verbal reports they brought back with them. Nick and Yoshi had assembled a unique record of a society devastated by a force unlike any other.

For days, Yoshi's hours of taped footage was aired on INN. Nick's verbal reports—kept on audiotapes—were also broadcast. No one had any doubt that Yoshi would win an Emmy Award. There was even talk that Nick might win one, too. He had already been offered a very lucrative book contract by Random House.

In the days alone in the "wilderness," Yoshi and Lieutenant Emiko Takado had grown very close.

After their return, Emiko had been called back to Japanese Self-Defense Force headquarters and reassigned. Now Yoshi just moped around the INN offices, missing her terribly. But at least he knew that, after the crisis was over, he would be reunited with her.

On the other hand, Brian noticed no progress between May McGovern and Nick. She still gave him the cold shoulder, and he still seemed to pretty much ignore her.

"Hey, Brian!" Nick greeted his roommate. "What's new?"

"Not much," Brian shrugged. "Still no word on Godzilla, even though the U.S. submarine fleet and the Russian Pacific fleet have both joined in the hunt."

"Don't worry," Nick replied. "Godzilla will show up. I've got a feeling in my gut."

Just then, an intern handed Brian an envelope. It had been hand-delivered (the Japanese postal service had suspended operations in Tokyo the day before—the same day the Japanese stock market had suspended trading). Brian saw his name scrawled on the white envelope, along with the address of INN, but nothing else.

Brian tore open the envelope.

Inside, he found a single sheet of paper. It was a letter from his still-missing uncle.

> *Dear Brian,*
> *Dr. Nobeyama and I have decided to act*
> *on our own. We've developed a lure, and*
> *are now installing it in a small private*

*airplane somewhere on the main
island—I'm sorry I can't tell you exactly
where.*

*Since the Japanese government—and
the governments of the world—seem
helpless to act, or are determined to do
the wrong thing, we are preparing our
own plan of defense.*

*Watch the skies. If Godzilla attacks
Tokyo, we will try to lead the monster to
the deepest part of the ocean. Then we'll
crash-dive our aircraft and sink, with the
lure, to the bottom of the Pacific Ocean.
We hope that Godzilla will follow us to
the deepest part of the Mariana Trench.*

*We are both fully aware that this is a
one-way trip. There is no way to carry
more fuel on such a small plane—and,
as I say, we are on our own in the belief
that this lure will be successful.*

*Whatever happens, remember that I'm
proud of you. Don't mourn for me or for
Dr. Nobeyama. I've spent my entire life
defending our country, and we are both
ready to die to defend the world—and for
what we believe in.*

*Remember, son, keep watching the
skies.*

Uncle Maxwell

Brian felt sick. Tears filled his eyes. *I've got to
find them...stop them!* Brian thought. But he
knew it was impossible. Even if he found his uncle

and the Japanese scientist, what could he say to convince them not to throw their lives away on an untried theory?

As Brian's mind raged, Nick looked down at his stricken friend.

"Hey, buddy," Nick asked. "What's the matter?"

But before Brian could reply, a commotion broke out in the newsroom. Brian and Nick rose to their feet to see what was going on. Everyone was staring at the television monitors. The regular programming had been replaced by an emergency broadcast.

"Emergency!" the voice on the television said. "Godzilla is in Tokyo Bay...repeat, Godzilla is in Tokyo Bay! Please evacuate the coastal areas in and around Tokyo. Repeat...Godzilla is in Tokyo Bay."

Outside, civil-defense sirens began to wail. Their shrill sound echoed through the streets of Tokyo. The eerie blare was a herald of disaster—Godzilla had returned!

While Tokyo prepared to wage war against a prehistoric monster, a war of another kind was brewing in the INN newsroom. This particular war began when a memo appeared on Nick's and Brian's computer screens—courtesy of electronic mail.

The memo, in essence, fired them both. And it was signed *Everett P. Endicott.*

The two young men met each other in the hallway outside the bureau chief's office. Without knocking, Brian and Nick stormed past a startled May McGovern and burst into Endicott's inner office.

"What's *this* all about?" Nick cried, waving a printout of the memo.

"Yeah," Brian sputtered, his indignation temporarily stealing his vocabulary.

Endicott rose ponderously from his chair and raised his arms. "I know you're upset, boys—"

"Don't give me that 'boys' crap, Chief!" Nick interrupted. "We 'boys' gave this network top news ratings for the months of May *and* June…"

"Which is why I issued that memo," Endicott shouted. His words temporarily silenced their protestations. The bureau chief stared at the two youths. "Sit down," he said.

When they were all seated, Endicott defended his actions. "Both of you have done enough," he told them. "You both have bright futures here at the Independent News Network—or anywhere else you choose. But I want you out of harm's way…I want you out of Tokyo."

"Well, that's not what *I* want," Nick replied. "I want the chance to go up on the tower and get some real, live air time!"

Endicott understood their disappointment. Using the last of their clout with the Japanese government, INN reporters were being permitted to observe Godzilla's attack—if it happened—from the observation deck of Tokyo Tower, the highest spot in the city.

Endicott himself had just assigned Max Hulse to do live, on-the-spot coverage of the event, which would be fed through a satellite uplink.

The bureau chief shook his head. "No," he said. "I won't permit it."

"Why not?" Brian asked.

"Because it's too dangerous," Endicott said simply.

"We've both faced danger before!" Nick cried.

Endicott nodded. "Yes, you have...but think about this. Max Hulse and those other men are going to be trapped on that tower if anything bad happens."

Nick's mouth snapped shut. He remembered his experience in the tiny factory tower. It was not something he wanted to repeat. "Max Hulse covered the Gulf War and the Middle East bombings in 1997," the bureau chief continued. "He *knows* the risks. You two seem to have forgotten that you're only interns...and you're young. I remember my youth well enough. You both think you're invincible."

"Okay." Nick relented. "But you can't just send us away."

"You're wrong about that," Endicott said with a thin smile. "In fifteen minutes, a private helicopter is landing on the helipad outside. I expect everyone to be on that aircraft and out of here. We'll leave behind a skeleton crew—one or two technicians—to man the uplinks, but the network wants everyone else out—*tonight!*—especially interns. It wouldn't look good for INN to put interns in harm's way."

When Nick and Brian left Endicott's office, the wind had pretty much been knocked out of their sails. As they headed back to their dorm rooms to pick up a few personal belongings, Nick looked around, trying to spot May.

She's probably getting packed, too, he told himself.

When the two youths reached the apartment they shared, Nick fumbled for his key. He pulled a car key out of his pocket instead.

"What's that?" Brian asked.

"Ahh, I used an INN car this morning," Nick replied. "I parked it in the basement garage, but I forgot to give the key back to Mr. Takao."

"Yeah, well, he won't be needing it now," Brian muttered. Then he froze, and so did Nick. They looked at each other.

"We have a *car!*" they said in unison.

While tanks and armored personnel carriers of the First Airborne Division—the unit traditionally charged with the duty of protecting the capital city—rushed to the shores of Tokyo Bay, mobs of frightened people fled the city.

From their balcony, Nick and Brian watched the chaos below as they made their plans. They both agreed to duck the evacuation helicopter. With an automobile at their disposal, they both felt that they could do their own reporting. It wouldn't be live, it wouldn't be broadcast as it was happening, but it would be *something*.

"I wish we could find Yoshi," Nick said. "I know how to use a video camera, but I'm no expert."

Brian nodded in agreement. "I think Yoshi is going to the tower," he said.

Nick paused and shook his head. *I hope he'll be okay.*

"Look!" Brian cried, pointing. "Here comes the helicopter!"

"Let's get out of here before someone tries to stop us." Nick quickly gathered up his video camera, his tape recorder, and plenty of tapes for both machines.

At the last minute, Brian grabbed his battery-powered portable television/radio and a police band receiver that was tuned to the emergency broadcast frequency.

"Good idea!" Nick said, spying the device. "Now we've got our own portable news van!"

"I'll drive," Brian insisted.

It took them a few minutes to sneak out of the INN building. There were security guys all over the place, herding people to the helipad. But eventually Nick and Brian made it to the garage. The red Toyota was just where Nick had left it.

"It's gassed and ready to go!" Nick said as they stowed their stuff and jumped inside. Brian checked the rear-view mirror and started the engine. Just then, they heard a clanking sound.

"Drive!" Nick screamed. "The guards are closing the security gates."

With a squeal of rubber, the Toyota peeled out. As they neared the exit, the metal grill gate began to descend.

"Hold on!" Brian cried as he stepped on the gas.

The car shot up the exit ramp and through the doorway. It just made it under the security gate—it was so close that the gate scraped some paint off the roof as it came down. As Brian turned the corner, Nick saw INN security men running after them.

"So long, suckers!" Nick cried triumphantly. "We've got an Emmy to pick up."

Brian laughed. As he sped through the deserted streets, he felt his heart pumping fast. He felt so *alive*.

Brian recalled the only other time he had felt like this. It was the day he'd made his first skydive. He remembered he was so scared, yet so exhilarated, too.

Then again, deep down inside, a nagging voice echoed a growing fear.

Who's really the sucker?

CHAPTER 20

GODZILLA RISING

June 18, 1998, 9:11 P.M.
Somewhere in the Roppongi District

They hadn't driven far before Brian pulled over to the curb. He switched off the engine and turned to his roommate. He and Nick exchanged puzzled glances.

"What now?" Brian asked.

"We wait," Nick replied. Then he placed the battery-powered television on the dashboard and began to channel-surf. He got mostly dead air.

"Try channel 57," Brian suggested. "It's been set to pick up INN satellite feeds."

"Cool!" Nick said as he flipped the channels. Max Hulse's bland face filled the tiny screen. "Talk to me, Maxie!" Nick quipped, turning up the sound.

"There is still no sign of Godzilla," the newscaster told the international audience. "No sign since he was seen in Tokyo Bay seven hours ago. Let's go to the tape…"

The image shifted, and Brian and Nick watched

the now-familiar shot of Godzilla rising from the waters of the bay.

"This shot was taken by a military spotter this afternoon. Evacuation of the areas near Tokyo Bay began by dusk. Now, in early evening, the city is nearly deserted.

"But *will* Godzilla come ashore? Will the monster destroy Tokyo for a *second* time?"

"Sheesh!" Nick said. "He sounds like he'd be disappointed if Godzilla *didn't* show up."

After that, Max Hulse switched over to Blackthorn Adams, who was reporting from Japanese military headquarters.

They listened as Adams launched into a review of Tokyo's defenses. He concentrated on the power grid that was built to protect the heart of Tokyo.

"After Godzilla's first assault," Adams explained, "the city planners built a series of high-tension wires around the heart of the city. These electrical wires carried power to a growing city…but the designers also planned for the unthinkable—the possible return of the monster Gojira, or a creature like it.

"Those power lines were built to handle much more electricity than necessary to power the city. If Godzilla ever returned, the grid would act as an electric fence that, it was hoped, would deter the monster from reaching the Imperial Palace and the business and commercial heart of Tokyo.

"Right now, even as I speak, the electrical defense grid is being readied."

Just then, Blackthorn Adams touched the headphone in his ear. He tilted his head and listened to a voice on the other end. "I'm told we have a live report coming in," he said into the camera. "It's from Ian Smelt and Gary Greg, who are stationed at the shore of Tokyo Bay. Can you hear me, Gary?"

As the two youths watched, the image shifted again. Gary Greg, formerly a weatherman for INN, had already begun his report.

"The monster has already destroyed the Shin Tatsumi Bridge and is heading for the heart of the city. Yes, I can see him now." The picture abruptly shifted away from the handsome newscaster and focused on a dark blot on the far horizon. The image was out of focus but soon became sharper.

It was Godzilla, rising out of Tokyo Bay and heading toward a ribbon of highway.

"Oh my god," Nick said, recognizing the location. "That's Expressway Number One!" he cried out in amazement. "Godzilla's only a few miles away from us."

Brian started the car's engine and drove down the narrow, deserted street toward the expressway.

While Gary Greg watched and Ian Smelt filmed, Godzilla stepped ashore near Expressway Number One. From their position on top of a modern apartment building, the newsmen watched the creature as he crashed through a dock area. Trucks and railroad cars were knocked aside as Godzilla lumbered toward the lights of the city.

While the former weatherman gave a running commentary, the British cameraman filmed the monster's arrival.

Godzilla paused. He seemed confused by his surroundings. Or perhaps the creature was dazzled by the lights of Tokyo, which spread out before him. He swiveled his massive head back and forth. His predatory eyes scanned the horizon. He seemed wary, as if he expected an enemy to attack.

It was then that a strange sound filled the creature's ears. The sound was not the unfamiliar wail of the sirens, which had been screaming since the monster came ashore.

It was a familiar sound—one that Godzilla had heard before.

"It's the rumble of tanks," Gary Greg said into the microphone he clutched with a sweaty hand. "Yes, over there!" he cried. "Dozens of tanks are rushing down the expressway…they're coming from both sides, converging on the monster."

Godzilla blinked his eyes, then stared down at the tiny objects that moved slowly toward him. His lips curled back, baring his teeth. A threatening growl rumbled in his throat.

The tanks slowed and halted. The turrets swiveled as the cannons aimed at the monster.

"According to briefings, these are Type 75 tanks," Gary Greg reported. "Elements of the First Airborne Division. They're aiming all their guns at Godzilla."

The tanks opened fire. Dozens of shells struck the monster, exploding against his hide. Godzilla whipped his tail back and forth angrily. The motion leveled three- and four-story buildings on both sides. Smoke and dust filled the air.

Immediately, Godzilla counterattacked. His

radioactive fire rained down on the armored vehicles. Many of the tanks backed away in time to avoid the heat ray.

Others weren't so lucky. Six tanks were reduced to radioactive slag, their crews vaporized. The rest of the tanks pulled back. They had tried to bluff Godzilla and failed.

Almost before it began, the attack ended.

"Now the tanks are pulling back," Gary Greg said as the image of the retreating tanks was beamed to a hundred countries.

"Will nothing stop this creature?"

As they raced through the streets toward the ramp to the expressway, Brian and Nick heard the sound of battle. Nick grabbed the television again and placed it on his lap.

"It looks like the tanks are retreating," Nick said as he watched the screen.

Just then, Godzilla's awful roar echoed through the steel and concrete canyons of the city. Brian slammed on the brakes. They stopped in the middle of a wide boulevard between two walls of skyscrapers. "Look up there!" Brian cried, pointing.

Nick looked. On a highway overpass just ahead of them, three tanks rumbled by at top speed. They were gone as quickly as they appeared.

Then something odd happened. The ground underneath the car began to shake.

"Oh-oh," Nick muttered.

Suddenly, the towering concrete and glass building to their right seemed to burst apart. Brian slammed the car in reverse and stepped on the gas. The tires spun, but the car only shimmied. Chunks of stone, shards of glass, and whole pieces of office furniture rained down on the street in front of them.

Some of the debris bounced toward the skidding car. Just then, the rubber caught the road, and the Toyota leaped backward.

It was not a moment too soon.

The huge front wall of the building hit the street with a deafening rumble. A fist-sized chunk of masonry struck the windshield, leaving a small diamond-shaped hole on the passenger side.

Brian continued to drive rapidly in reverse, putting as much distance as possible between himself and the crumbling building. Finally, he lost control of the car. The Toyota hopped the curb and sideswiped an orange pay phone. Brian slammed on the brakes and the engine stalled.

They watched, paralyzed, as Godzilla's massive foot crashed down on the street where, moments before, their car had sat. Almost casually, the monster brushed tons of rubble aside and slammed against the apartment complex on the opposite side of the street.

That building, too, tumbled like a house of cards.

As the apartment building crashed to the ground, the air was filled with choking dust and clouds of smoke. In seconds, Nick and Brian were blinded. They sat, quaking helplessly in the front seat of the car, until the ground finally ceased to rumble and the monster moved on.

*   *   *

"Godzilla is laying waste to the Shibaura section of Tokyo," Max Hulse informed his millions of viewers. From his vantage point on Tokyo Tower, all he could really see with the naked eye was the glowing fires in Godzilla's wake and the occasional flash of a distant explosion.

But thanks to dozens of cameras in helicopters that crisscrossed the skies over the city, the rampage was being taped from many different angles. All of the visual images were being fed to INN headquarters, and to Hulse and his remote team on Tokyo Tower.

"As you can see, the creature's advance through the city is not being opposed by the military." Hulse cleared his throat and paused for a moment.

"I've just been informed that Godzilla is nearing a section of high-tension wires," he told the viewers.

"In a few moments, we'll know if the so-called electric fence will keep Godzilla out."

Godzilla approached the steel structure warily. The creature instinctively sensed the energy that coursed through the nearly invisible wires. The creature halted. His feral head turned left, then right. But there was no opening in the wall of electrically charged wires.

Cautiously, Godzilla moved forward. His body made contact with the high-tension wires in several places.

Molten fire shot through the monster's body. Godzilla twisted his neck in spasms of pain. Bellowing, he thrashed his tail, striking the base of one of the towers.

The structure began to collapse, breaking some of the wires. Sparks exploded as the wires struck buildings, trees, and abandoned vehicles.

The pain was lessened, and Godzilla pushed through the barrier. Sparks ran up and down his body. The creature opened his mouth and groaned in agony.

Then the spikes on Godzilla's back began to glow. Radioactive fire built up in the creature's chest. He twisted his head and extended his long neck. A hot jet blasted from the monster's gaping mouth and struck the nearest electrical tower. The steel framework began to glow, then melt.

The tower collapsed into a heap of molten metal. Godzilla blinked and reared back. Another blast of radioactive fire melted a second steel tower.

Godzilla's roar of triumph rolled over the helpless city.

There was so much dust and debris covering their Toyota that Brian had to get out and wipe it off so he could see out of the windshield. Nick hopped out too. He was clutching the portable television.

After the terrible sound of Godzilla's passing, the silence in the streets was eerie. Far away, the civil-defense sirens still wailed. Closer to them, the alarm from a long-abandoned car warbled. There was no sign of any other human being.

"Come on," Brian said after he cleared the windows. "Let's go."

"Wait a minute," Nick replied. "I think I'm getting something...Okay!"

Max Hulse's voice, sounding tinny over the tiny

speakers, droned on. "We're back, ladies and gentlemen," he said apologetically. "When the power grid was broken, we temporarily lost power. Now our emergency generators are up and running. Again, I apologize for the temporary loss of power, and thank you for staying with us."

"And not switching over to CNN," Nick added cynically.

They sat on the hood, listening to the report. After a few minutes, Godzilla's image filled the screen once again.

"The creature is approaching Expressway Number Two in the Shiba district," Hulse announced. "He is very close to our remote broadcast center here in Tokyo Tower. Yes, I can see the creature out the window, but he still seems far away."

"Do you know how to get to Shiba?" Brian asked.

"Yeah," Nick replied. "But we should take Sakurada-Dori, there's less traffic..."

Brian looked at his friend. "Nick, are you crazy? The city's deserted."

"Yeah," Nick snorted. "Except for those *tanks* on the expressway."

CHAPTER 21

HOME AGAIN

June 18, 1998, 11:20 P.M.
On the edge of Shiba Park
Tokyo, Japan

It took longer than they expected to drive to Godzilla's location. Nick gave pretty good directions, but they found their way was constantly blocked—sometimes by debris from shattered buildings, but mostly by abandoned vehicles. They detoured a number of times before finally reaching the wide street called Sakurada-Dori.

The campus of Keio University was abandoned, but as they drove past Senba Hospital, they saw the first signs of other human beings. The hospital buildings were brightly lit, and a number of ambulances rushed by, their sirens warbling.

When they reached the ramp to Expressway Number Two, Nick looked up from his map. "Turn right!" he cried, pointing. The red Toyota's tires skidded as Brian spun around the corner. As they approached another overpass—the map said it was Hibiya-Dori—they saw a bright flash to their right. Since the expressway was pretty much empty,

Brian stopped the car in the center of the road.

They watched as Godzilla emerged from the smoke and haze that hung over the Shiba district. They had a great view of the Tokyo Grand Hotel— right before Godzilla leveled it. Then the monster turned and seemed to approach them.

Brian quickly threw the car into reverse and backed up until he was under the Hibiya-Dori overpass. Then he turned off the engine. They watched as Godzilla stepped onto the expressway, shattering light poles and cracking the pavement. Again, the ground shook under the car, and dust and debris rained down on the Toyota from the overpass above.

When the monster's tail disappeared from view, Brian started the car again and warily drifted out from under the overpass. He and Nick watched Godzilla's back as it moved away from them.

"Try the television," Brian suggested.

Nick plopped the TV on the dashboard and tuned in to INN. Max Hulse was still giving a running commentary, but this time he wasn't using a remote camera. Godzilla was entering Shiba Park, approaching an ancient Japanese shrine.

"Godzilla is clearly visible from our vantage point here in Tokyo Tower," Hulse was saying. "He is approaching Zojoji Temple, a national landmark."

The temple appeared on the television screen. It was a small building with slate gray tiles on its roof and aged red lacquer walls. As they watched, Godzilla's leg seemed to brush against the centuries-old structure, and it collapsed into a cloud of dust.

The monster paused and bellowed out a roar. He stood in the middle of a manicured parkland. His swishing tail flattened trees and shrubs. His massive feet left deep footprints in the well-kept grasslands and gardens.

Then Godzilla blinked. He focused his eyes on a brightly lit structure that was even taller than he was. With a roar of challenge, the creature began to move toward Tokyo Tower.

Mike Lacey, the INN remote producer stationed on the observation deck of Tokyo Tower, tore his eyes off the monitor screens of his portable workstation.

"I need another cameraman," he cried. "It looks like Godzilla is coming this way."

The assistant producer, a young woman from Alabama, shook her head. "The only other cameraman we've got is Yoshi Masahara—and I just sent him below to iron out a technical glitch in our satellite feed truck." She paused. "Do you want me to call him back?" she asked.

Lacey looked down at his monitor again. Godzilla was heading right for them.

"Forget it," he said finally. "And I think you should leave too..."

She opened her mouth to protest, but the producer interrupted her before she could speak. "Leave now, and take everyone else with you. We'll make do with Max and the cameraman we already have."

The woman looked at her boss. "But—" she muttered.

"Don't argue—*go!*" Mike Lacey cried, then turned his back on her and went to work again.

The woman faced the members of her technical crew. "Okay, people," she said. "You heard the boss. Get onto the elevators...*Now!*"

Brian was driving again. He warily circled Shiba Park, keeping one eye on Godzilla and the other on the sky.

Keep watching the sky! his uncle had told him in the letter. But so far, Brian had seen nothing. Following Nick's directions, Brian left the expressway and drove along the residential streets that bordered Shiba Park.

"It looks like Godzilla is heading for Tokyo Tower," Brian said ominously. Both of them thought about Yoshi, but neither voiced their fears about their friend's safety.

They circled around the Tokyo Prince Hotel. The old stone structure had an enormous parking lot surrounding it. Brian pulled into the center of the almost empty lot. He and Nick jumped out of their car and climbed onto its roof.

They watched as Godzilla approached the orange tower that loomed over him.

Nick fiddled with the television and a picture appeared. It was a shot from the cameras in the tower. Godzilla seemed to lock his predatory eyes on the camera itself as he moved inexorably forward.

Max Hulse continued to give commentary, ignoring the deadly approach of Godzilla.

"Godzilla is approaching the tower now," Hulse

said in a calm, professional voice. "If he destroys this tower, we will certainly loose transmitting capabilities, but I am sure that other INN facilities will fill in for us."

"Stop talking and get out of there!" Nick cried at the image on the screen.

Brian and Nick moved their eyes from the image on the screen to the actual vision of the creature as he approached the tower. Even at this distance, the earth shook and Godzilla's roar battered their ears.

"It seems that Godzilla is intent on destruction," Max Hulse said calmly. "He is approaching Tokyo Tower. Let's get another shot of this." Hulse disappeared and was replaced by a shot of Godzilla. The creature stared right into the camera lens with a cold, reptilian gaze.

"The creature is very close now," Hulse intoned. "He's reaching out his arm—"

Suddenly, the image on the screen shook. Nick and Brian looked up to see Godzilla grabbing the tower and shaking it with both massive arms.

"The tower is swaying," Hulse reported, a professional to the last. "I think it will give way soon. This is Max Hulse, in Tokyo, Japan, signing off—"

Suddenly, the screen went white. Brian looked up and saw Tokyo Tower bend, then shatter. The upper half of the tower slowly tilted, then broke loose.

As they watched in horror, the upper half of the steel structure crashed to the streets below. Godzilla roared again and grappled with the twisted metal as if it were a living opponent. The monster continued to smash its clawed fists against the tower until the entire structure was reduced to a pile of twisted metal.

"Oh, God," Nick gasped. "Poor Max—"

Brian blinked back tears. "I just hope Yoshi got out of there," he muttered.

"Nobody got out of there," Nick replied.

As they watched, Godzilla, his rage spent, moved away from the ruins of Tokyo Tower and toward the city beyond.

Nick and Brian were quiet for a few moments. Then Brian looked at his friend.

"Where do you think Godzilla is headed now?" he asked.

Nick squinted into the distance. "Toward Roppongi—and home," he said grimly.

"Then let's go," Brian said, jumping off the roof.

"Okay," Nick agreed. "But it's *my* turn to drive."

On the other side of Tokyo, on the tarmac of Haneda Airport, sat twelve military helicopters. As their rotors were revved up by the ground crews, the pilots and weapons officers listened to a final briefing.

The helicopters were U.S.-built McDonnell Douglas AH-64A Apache attack helicopters—perhaps the most advanced attack chopper in the world. These aircraft were manned by members of the Japanese Self-Defense Force.

Trained by the United States military for night fighting, each Apache crew was supplied with an integrated Pilot's Night Vision System. This optical system, which involved a futuristic helmet called an IHADSS (Integrated Helmet And Display

Sighting System), enabled the helicopter pilot and weapons officer to have a clear field of vision, even on the darkest nights.

"I hope you will not have to rely on night vision," their commanding officer, General Sato, told his men as they awaited takeoff.

"So far, Tokyo is still lit, and you should have no trouble spotting your target."

As the general briefed his men, technicians were replacing the sixteen Hellfire missiles that were fired from pods on either side of the Apache with a new type of weapon.

"We have replaced the explosive warhead of the Hellfire missiles with a newly developed tranquilizing agent," General Sato informed them.

"This substance has been designed to knock the creature out. The substance is harmless to human beings and to the environment—but it should be effective against Godzilla, if our scientists are correct."

As the general outlined the plan of attack, the ground crews finished loading the new type of missiles. When he saw the 'go' signal from the ground controller, the general finished his briefing.

"Do your duty!" he said, gazing at his soldiers with pride.

The helicopter crews shouted in unison as they raised their arms above their heads. Then they boarded their aircraft with grim determination.

One by one, the Apaches began to lift off the tarmac in a cloud of dust.

When all twelve Apaches were airborne, they joined up over Haneda Airport and headed toward the heart of Tokyo.

* * *

"This area looks awfully familiar," Nick said, alarm in his voice. Brian blinked. He didn't know how Nick could find any familiar landmarks in the ruins they had been driving past for the last ten minutes.

For over an hour, they had paced Godzilla's advance. Usually, they drove their car parallel to Godzilla, keeping one eye on the monster and the other on the road and the direction they were taking.

In the last half-hour, Godzilla seemed to have doubled back the way he'd come. Following him, Nick and Brian found themselves in the heart of the destruction.

At first they just smelled smoke. Then they began to pass buildings that were ablaze. A few times, they had to detour around crumbled buildings and rubble-strewn streets. Once they stumbled upon a fire truck and a horde of firemen battling a tremendous high-rise fire.

Fortunately, Godzilla had not employed his radioactive fire since destroying the power lines. Though burning buildings were plentiful, most of the city remained free of fire damage.

Nick had slowed down considerably since they reentered the area of destruction. He often had to maneuver to avoid debris, and he even hopped the curb once or twice to get around chunks of concrete.

Once, he had to swerve to avoid a corpse. Brian thought about stopping and checking on the victim, but it was painfully obvious that the person was dead. No one could survive such wounds.

The sound of destruction still rang around them—interspersed with the wail of civil-defense sirens and the blare of ambulances and other emergency vehicles. Occasionally, Godzilla could be heard, too. His bell-like roar rang through the shattered streets of Tokyo.

Once in a while, Brian and Nick would stop and try to find something on the television. But when Tokyo Tower had been leveled, it had also brought down the microwave transmitters at the top. All the two of them got on the screen was dead air.

When they tried the radio, all they could hear were local stations. Neither of them could speak Japanese well enough to understand the announcer's rapid-fire speech.

And so they just drove. The destruction was so monumental, so complete, that they soon grew numb to the sight of it. Silently, they pressed on. They continued to follow the monster, but no longer knew why.

Neither of them had used the camera or the tape recorder since their "adventure" began.

"Oh, no!" Nick cried, slamming on the brakes. Brian, who did not have his seat belt fastened, was thrown forward.

"What the—" he exclaimed. Nick was staring at the shattered block in front of them.

"Look!" Nick cried, pointing. At first, Brian just saw more destruction. Broken concrete, twisted steel girders, glass and debris scattered about. Down near the end of the block, a whole apartment complex had fallen to one side. It looked eerily familiar.

"That's the INN dorm!" Brian said. He shifted his gaze, searching for the INN building itself. Where the building once stood, there was only a three-story pile of rubble. Nick put his foot on the gas and they warily drove toward the building they had once called home.

"I see somebody!" Brian cried, pointing. There was a dirty, ragged figure sitting on the curb. Brian couldn't see the man's face, which was buried in his hands, but the man seemed oddly familiar.

"That's the chief!" Nick cried in shock and surprise. He stopped the car and jumped out. Brian quickly followed. Both youths ran to Endicott's side.

"Hey, chief," Nick said, shaking the man's shoulders. "Are you okay?"

Everett P. Endicott slowly lifted his head. His face was streaked with soot, and his eyes were oddly vacant.

"Mr. Gordon," he replied dazedly. "We were looking for you earlier…"

"What happened?" Nick demanded. "What were you doing here?"

The bureau chief blinked. "Someone had to stay behind and man the studio," he said. "I couldn't ask anyone else to do it…"

Endicott's faraway stare remained fixed as he relived the events of the past hours.

"Everyone had left on the helicopter," he droned on in an unemotional voice. "Everyone but you and Mr. Shimura. I took over control duties. I kept the satellite feed going. Then Godzilla destroyed Tokyo Tower." The portly man began to sob.

"I watched poor Max die," he said as tears

streamed down his chubby cheeks. "Then May came in and said we had to go...that Godzilla was coming."

"May!" Nick cried. "May is here, too?" He looked around. "Where is she?" he demanded, shaking Endicott's shoulders. The man shook his head and pointed to the ruins of the building behind them.

"She said she'd meet me in the lobby, but when I got down there..." His voice drifted off and his eyes stared forward, unseeing.

"He's in shock," Brian muttered.

"We've got to find May!" Nick cried again. "We've got to find her!" With that, Nick ran toward the ruins of the INN building, screaming May McGovern's name over and over again.

Brian didn't want to leave the bureau chief, but he also wanted to help find May—if she was still alive. Then, at that moment, he heard the sound of helicopters—lots of helicopters.

He looked up as twelve Apache attack helicopters flew over their heads like a horde of angry wasps. They headed directly toward Godzilla, who was still moving, blocks away.

In the town of Kakegawa, less than a hundred miles from Tokyo, a single-engine Cessna sat alone on the runway of the local airport. Light spilled from a nearby hangar, where two men busily worked on an electronic device the size of a small suitcase. A burst of weird, high-pitched sound sometimes filled the hangar as they tinkered with the machine.

"How's this?" Admiral Willis asked as he adjusted

the frequency again. He threw a switch on the side of the device and another burst of noise echoed throughout the huge enclosure.

Dr. Nobeyama looked at his notes and nodded enthusiastically. "That's perfect," he said. "According to my data, the lure is now set at the precise frequency of Godzilla's own brainwaves."

"Then I think it's time to go fishin'," the admiral said, shutting off the sound machine. "Let's install this baby in the airplane and get out of here."

While Admiral Willis lifted the device, Dr. Nobeyama closed his notebook and placed it on a table piled with papers, graphs, and blueprints.

As the two men left the hangar and approached the Cessna, a jeep suddenly appeared at the other end of the airport. The vehicle, which had the markings of the Japanese Self-Defense Force painted on it, raced across the tarmac. With a final squeal of tires on pavement, the jeep skidded to a halt in front of them.

Lieutenant Emiko Takado hastily exited the vehicle and blocked their way. She put her hands on her hips and stared at the two men.

"Emiko, what are you doing here?" Dr. Nobeyama asked, surprised by his assistant's sudden appearance.

"I'm here to stop you both from killing yourselves," she replied, her eyes flashing. "I know what you're planning."

Admiral Willis, still holding the device, stepped up to her. "It's the only way to stop Godzilla," he said evenly.

"NO!" she cried, shaking her head. "If the lure

really *does* work, then you must tell the government…or the military….Surely someone will listen?"

"There is no other way," Dr. Nobeyama said. "We have tried to convince the authorities, but they would not listen. Now it is up to us."

Admiral Willis walked past the young woman and approached the airplane. He climbed into the Cessna's cockpit and began bolting the device to the dashboard. Lieutenant Takado and Dr. Nobeyama followed behind.

"Please, Admiral," Lieutenant Takado persisted. "This plan is suicide!"

"The lure works," the American replied as he continued to install the device. "Dr. Nobeyama and I intend to use it to draw Godzilla to the deepest part of the Pacific Ocean. As I said before, it's the only way…"

"But why don't you just lead the monster out to sea," she argued. "Surely, when the military knows that the device works—"

Dr. Nobeyama put his hand on her shoulder. "No, Emiko," he said, interrupting her. "If we hesitate, more people will die…"

"Then just throw the device overboard when you're out to sea," she said. "Turn the plane around and fly back to Japan."

"I'm sorry, Emiko. It's a one-way trip," Admiral Willis answered. "We have enough fuel to lead Godzilla all the way to the Mariana Trench. But not enough to get back."

Emiko's eyes filled with tears.

Dr. Nobeyama sighed. "Don't be sad," he said.

"We've made our decision, and have no regrets.

"My notes are inside the hangar. Give them to the military when we are gone. Whether we fail or succeed, perhaps they can use this knowledge in some way."

Lieutenant Takado was silent for a moment. "I will miss you both," she whispered finally.

Dr. Nobeyama smiled. "I think you've wasted enough time working for an old man like me. I also think that Yoshi Masahara is a fine man, and you will both be very happy."

The Cessna's engine sputtered to life. Dr. Nobeyama climbed into the cockpit next to Admiral Willis. The two men waved good-bye as the airplane began to move across the tarmac.

Lieutenant Emiko Takado watched as the Cessna taxied down the runway, its running lights blinking. Then it shot into the sky and disappeared in the darkness. In less than a minute, the sound of the engine faded, too, and Emiko was alone.

CHAPTER 22

HELICOPTER ATTACK

June 19, 1998, 1:23 A.M.
Somewhere over Tokyo

Lieutenant Ogata in Apache One radioed his squadron.

"The creature is below us now," he said. "Prepare to attack!" The other pilots acknowledged his command and formed up behind his aircraft.

When all was in readiness, he spoke to his weapons officer, who rode in the cockpit behind him. "I will sweep low, between those two rows of skyscrapers," he said. "Fire when you are certain you will not miss."

Lieutenant Ogata hoped that the missiles would be effective, but despite his commander's assurances that the tranquilizer in their tips was powerful, and posed no danger to the human population, he wanted to take no chances.

"Make every shot count!" he said. Then he guided his helicopter down toward Godzilla.

"May!" Nick shouted. "Can you hear me?"

He stumbled through debris and tripped over chunks of concrete. He looked all around, searching for any clue to her whereabouts. His search was unfocused and unplanned—it was born of desperation, not logic.

I have to find her! a voice inside his head screamed.

Nick heard the sound of rotors overhead but ignored them. His only concern was finding May. As he climbed over the rubble, Nick's foot caught in a long steel cable and he tripped. He landed hard, falling against a huge steel box.

No! Not a box...it's the elevator. For a second, hope surged. He grabbed a piece of concrete and banged on the side of the shattered elevator.

"May!" he screamed. "Are you in there?" He dropped the chunk of concrete and put his ear against the steel door.

Yes! He almost cried out loud. *Someone is definitely inside.*

Nick put his fingers on the door frame and tried to slide the doors open. It was impossible. The doors were partially crushed, and seemed to be frozen in place. He kicked the door in frustration.

And someone cried out from inside. It was a woman's voice, muffled and indistinct...but alive!

He thought fast. There must be an escape hatch on top of the elevator!

Nick jumped to the roof of the steel box. He kicked dirt and debris away and searched for something that looked like a door.

Yes! There it was!

The hatch was secured in place by four screws

in each corner. Nick didn't have a screwdriver—and he didn't have time to look for one. He fumbled inside his pocket until he found a coin. He fit it into the groove of one screw and began to turn. His fingers were soon sore and bloody, but one by one, the screws were coming off.

Lieutenant Ogata's Apache attack helicopter dived out of the sky toward the lumbering monster called Godzilla. He depressed the button on the control stick and the whole aircraft shuddered as the chin-mounted chain gun erupted. A stream of steel-jacketed shells slammed into Godzilla's body.

Behind the lieutenant, the weapons officer depressed a trigger and, one by one, all sixteen missiles left their pods and struck.

Godzilla bellowed in rage. Fire danced across the creature's chest as the missiles hit his hide. There was no explosion—nor did Ogata expect any.

When the missiles reached their target, Ogata swerved the Apache and shot up and over a row of buildings. He put the skyscrapers between his aircraft and the monster.

But Godzilla would not be stopped once he had spotted his prey. Without hesitation, he slammed against the steel-and-glass structure and crashed right through the center of the block-long building.

But Godzilla was too late. Lieutenant Ogata had flown his Apache out of harm's way.

As the monster roared and bellowed, another Apache took the first one's place. It too fired its missiles, all of which struck Godzilla's thick hide. But this time, Godzilla opened his mouth. Blue fire shot up his dorsal spines and a hot jet of flame engulfed the second Apache. It vanished in a huge fireball.

Undeterred by the fate of their comrades—or the fact that the tranquilizer was having no noticeable effect—the pilots of the third and fourth Apaches dived down for the attack.

His fingers slick with sweat, Nick Gordon ripped the emergency hatch off the top of the elevator car. "May!" he screamed as he peered down into the dark elevator.

"Nick," a voice from the darkness sobbed. "Is it really you?"

Nick scrambled through the hatch and lowered himself into the elevator car. As his eyes got used to the darkness, he saw a form huddled in the corner. He reached down and lifted May in his arms. For a few moments, they did not move, they did not speak. They just held each other.

"Hey!" Brian cried from outside the hatch. "Is anybody in there?"

"Yeah!" Nick replied, relief in his voice. "It's May…and she's all right. Help me get her out of here."

Over Tokyo, and between the high buildings, a battle raged. It was human and machine against monster. The monster was winning.

"Situation report!" Lieutenant Ogata demanded from his Apache high over Tokyo.

"We lost Two and Five," a voice crackled in his headphones. "We've fired all of our missiles into the monster. The tranquilizer is not working."

Lieutenant Ogata cursed.

"Should we attack with machine guns?" the other man asked his commander. Lieutenant Ogata shook his head bitterly.

"*No!*" he cried into his microphone. "Break off the attack and regroup over the city. There is nothing more we can do now."

As Brian and Nick helped a shaken and bruised May down from the ruins, the Apaches flew overhead again. This time they were going in the opposite direction.

The two youths exchanged glances.

"Another attack has failed," Nick said. "I guess there is really no hope now…"

But Brian did not reply. Instead he cocked his head. He could swear he heard the sound of an engine. *Yes!* As he turned his eyes to the sky, a light aircraft flew overhead, heading directly for Godzilla's location.

"Maybe we *do* have a chance, after all," Brian whispered cryptically. Nick and May both looked at him with puzzled expressions.

"Let me tell you about a letter I got earlier today," Brian said.

Inside the private airplane over Tokyo, Admiral Maxwell Willis peered out the window at the city far below. He banked, dipping his wing. The airplane turned and flew right over the location of

INN headquarters. The admiral could see that the whole block was in ruins.

"It's time to activate the lure," Dr. Nobeyama said from the seat beside him.

The admiral smiled at his old friend. "Are you ready to do this?" he asked.

The Japanese scientist shrugged his shoulders. "It's *bushido*—our duty," he replied.

"And our honor, too," the admiral said simply.

The airplane banked low and made a pass over Godzilla's head. The monster seemed oblivious to their presence.

"I will activate the lure." Dr. Nobeyama flicked a switch. "Now!"

A keening, high-pitched wail that was barely audible to human ears filled the air from a dozen speakers embedded in the fuselage. The admiral banked the aircraft again and made a second pass over the monster.

To his amazement, Godzilla froze in mid-stride. The monster looked up, scanning the sky for the source of the sound. As the aircraft turned again, Godzilla turned with it.

"It's working!" the admiral cried.

"You are surprised?" Dr. Nobeyama said, lifting one eyebrow.

The admiral chuckled. "And why shouldn't I be?" he said. "I remember that little wind tunnel experiment a few years back…"

"Your design was all wrong!" Dr. Nobeyama insisted.

"Oh, no." Admiral Willis shook his head. "My design was fine. Your *calculations* were wrong!"

"Never!" the Japanese scientist said indignantly.

As they argued good-naturedly, the admiral banked the airplane, turned, and headed toward Tokyo Bay and the Pacific Ocean beyond. And like a fish on the end of a fisherman's line, Godzilla followed.

Nick shook his head in disbelief. May, too, had a look of wonder on her pretty face. Everett Endicott, still suffering from a mild case of shock, stared vacantly at the sky as the airplane, carrying Admiral Willis, Dr. Nobeyama, and the lure, flew over their heads.

Like a docile lamb, Godzilla walked along behind. The ground shook as the creature, drawn compulsively to the lure devised by the two men, increased his pace to keep up with the airplane.

"I can't believe it worked!" Nick exclaimed.

"That's my uncle," Brian replied.

"You've got to tell the world!" May insisted.

"I sure would like to," Brian agreed. "But all communications are out."

"Unless you've got a satellite truck, the hottest story of the year is going to remain our little secret," Nick said with disgust.

At that moment, a most amazing thing happened. Brian heard another engine—a truck engine. Nick, who was whispering to May, looked up when he heard the sound. Even Endicott snapped out of his stupor.

They looked down the block as a huge white van with big INN letters on the side rounded the corner. Behind the wheel sat Yoshi Masahara; the blond network producer from Alabama was in the passenger seat.

The van pulled up to the curb and the side door swung open. Six technicians hopped out and stretched. Yoshi and the woman also jumped out. Yoshi ran up and greeted them.

There was much backslapping, and high fives all around. Brian told everyone about his uncle, the airplane, and the lure that even now drew Godzilla farther and farther from the shores of Japan.

The mood of celebration was suddenly shattered as a commanding voice broke through the conversation. All eyes turned to see Everett P. Endicott on his feet and glaring at them.

"What is going on here?" he demanded. "We have a satellite truck, a power generator, uplink capability, a damn fine cameraman, and a producer—and two honest-to-God reporters—here."

He paused. "Let's get to *work*, people! We have news to report."

Everyone jumped into action. Within minutes, they had established communications with INN stateside and established a satellite feed. Yoshi manned the camera, and Brian and Nick prepared statements.

The woman from Alabama cleaned the two youths up as well as she could. She even produced some makeup from her purse.

Finally, all was in readiness.

"Okay, we're going on the air worldwide—live—in sixty seconds," the woman said. "Get to your places."

"You've got the big story," Nick said to Brian. "I'll go on first and set the stage…Then you can tell the world about Dr. Nobeyama's invention—and your uncle's courage."

"It's a deal," Brian said, feeling a little nervous.

"Ten seconds!" the woman shouted.

Nick took his place in front of the camera. He gripped the microphone and cleared his throat. Then he stole a glance at May and Brian.

"Three…two…one…*go!*"

Nick stood up straight, looked into the camera, and spoke.

"The ruins you see behind me were once a great city," he said in a somber tone.

"The creature that caused the destruction is gone for now, but the damage Godzilla left in his wake will take decades to rebuild…" Nick paused dramatically.

"*This* is Tokyo…"

EPILOGUE

June 19, 1998, 9:11 A.M.
Somewhere in the Pacific Ocean

High above the Pacific, hundreds of miles from the nearest shore, the tiny airplane's engine sputtered and died. Its fuel exhausted, the plane glided for a few more miles, then drifted down until it finally hit the waves and broke apart.

The pieces floated for a few minutes, then sank.

The lure that compelled Godzilla to follow the airplane continued to function. Powered by batteries, the device was designed to emit the sound for many, many weeks—perhaps even months.

As the lure sank beneath the waves, Godzilla happily went with it. Soon, the monster was following the machine to the very bottom of the deepest part of the ocean.

Perhaps the monster will rest there forever. Or perhaps, at some future time, Godzilla will return again…

ABOUT THE AUTHOR

MARC CERASINI saw his first Godzilla movie at the age of seven and instantly joined the ranks of obsessed Godzilla fans the world over. Through the years, he has lived out a quest to collect everything and anything Godzilla and has amassed an impressive menagerie of rare Japanese Godzilla figures.

In addition to being a giant G fan, Marc is a writer and screenwriter of diverse abilities. He is the author of numerous fantasy short stories as well as the *New York Times* best-selling biography *O. J. Simpson: American Hero, American Tragedy.* He has co-authored the best-selling *Tom Clancy Companion* and the critically acclaimed title *Robert E. Howard*. In addition, Marc has written a number of children's books, including the Random House Bullseye adaptation of Victor Hugo's *The Hunchback of Notre Dame.*

Marc is a native of Pittsburgh, Pennsylvania, and now makes his home in New York City. He will soon be writing a Godzilla page for an Internet site on the World Wide Web.

Look for more exciting
GODZILLA™ reading...

Here is a thrilling retelling of Godzilla's *first* appearance in Tokyo, Japan, as seen through the eyes of three children...

On a stormy night in a remote Japanese fishing village, Yukio, Lily, and little Shiro awake to find everyone in their village fleeing for the safety of the mountains. Left behind, these siblings take refuge from the storm in a nearby cave, then watch in amazement as a dinosaur monster, as tall as a skyscraper, wades to shore and tears their village to pieces. They are among the first human beings to actually *see* this incredible beast!

Everyone wants to hear their story—from the military and the politicians to the press—but few seem to believe them...until Godzilla *himself* arrives in Tokyo. The rest of the world now gasps in fear as it sees for itself the most awesome creature ever to walk the Earth!

GODZILLA™ LIVES!

Look for these titles, available wherever books are sold.

OR

You can send in this coupon (with check or money order)
and have the books mailed directly to you!

❑ *Godzilla™: King of the Monsters* (0-679-88220-0)
by Scott Ciencin $3.99

❑ *Godzilla™ Returns* (0-679-88221-9)
by Marc Cerasini $4.99

❑ *Godzilla™ Saves America: A Monster Showdown in 3-D!*
(0-679-88079-8)
by Marc Cerasini, illustrated by
Tom Morgan & Paul Mounts $11.99

❑ *Godzilla™ Versus Gigan™ and the Smog Monster*
(0-679-88344-4)
by Alice Alfonsi, illustrated by Motown Animation $3.99

❑ *Godzilla™ on Monster Island* (0-679-88080-1)
by Jacqueline Dwyer, illustrated by
Tom Morgan & Paul Mounts $3.99

Subtotal	$	
Shipping and handling	$	3.00
Sales tax (where applicable)	$	
Total amount enclosed	$	

Name _____

Address _____

City _____ **State** _____ **Zip** _____

Make your check or money order (no cash or C.O.D.s) payable to
Random House and mail to Bullseye Mail Sales, 400 Hahn Road,
Westminster, MD 21157.

Prices and numbers subject to change without notice. Valid in U.S. only.
All orders subject to availability. Please allow 4 to 6 weeks for delivery.

Need your books even faster? Call toll-free 1-800-793-2665
to order by phone and use your major credit card.
Please mention interest code 002-10 to expedite your order.